# Armada

# Armada

## Thomas Hobbs, England 1587-1588

by Jim Eldridge

■ SCHOLASTIC

# To my wife, Lynne

While the events described and some of the characters in this book may be based on actual historical events and real people, Thomas Hobbes is a fictional character, created by the author, and his story is a work of fiction.

Scholastic Children's Books
Commonwealth House, 1–19 New Oxford Street,
London, WC1A 1NU, UK
A division of Scholastic Ltd
London ~ New York ~ Toronto ~ Sydney ~ Auckland
Mexico City ~ New Delhi ~ Hong Kong

Published in the UK by Scholastic Ltd, 2002

Copyright © Jim Eldridge, 2002

ISBN 0 439 98112 3

Typeset by Falcon Oast Graphic Art Ltd, East Hoathly, East Sussex
Printed and bound in Great Britain by Mackays of Chatham Limited, Chatham, Kent
Cover image: Detail from Portrait of Don Giovanni de' Medici by Agnolo Bronzino.
Ashmolean Museum, Oxford, UK/Bridgeman Art Library
Background image: Detail from the Spanish Armada by Norman Wilkinson. Mary
Evans Picture Library

2 4 6 8 10 9 7 5 3 1

The right of Jim Eldridge to be identified as the author of this work has been
asserted by him in accordance with the Copyright, Designs and Patents Act, 1988.

## 1588

In this year of Our Lord 1588 and in the reign of our blessed Queen Elizabeth, I do put my mark to this paper and swear that this story set out by me, is true. It is the tale of how I, Thomas Hobbs, now aged fourteen years and nine months, of the City of London, did join the English fleet that destroyed the great Spanish Armada and did help save this country of ours from sovereign Spanish rule.

I was thirteen years old and living with my mam and my dad, my sister Mary and my baby brother Daniel in Eastcheap in the city of London. There had been more of us children – four more, so I once heard Mam say – but the others had died as babies.

Our home was two rooms in a large building called Garlands, which had been a manor house in better days some hundred years before. With so many people squashed into the building, sometimes two families to a room, it was hard to think that once fine Lords and Ladies had lived there. We were lucky to have two rooms to ourselves. This was because my dad worked as a day butcher in Cheapside and so could afford more space for us. Usually my dad worked for Butcher Perkin, but when he could not employ him, Dad would find work with any other butcher who would take him. All the butchers knew my dad because they were all next to each other in Cheapside. It is that way in London: every trade congregating together. In Bucklesbury are all the herb sellers, with the scent of herbs so strong it would make anyone feel faint. At Smithfield is the market for horses and cattle, with great flies that buzz and bite and leave red marks on the skin of anyone unlucky enough to have one land on them.

According to my dad, Smithfield was the place where they burnt Protestant heretics when Catholic Queen Mary, our Queen's sister, was alive. More than 300 of them were burnt up and down the country. When Dad started to talk about things like the troubles between Catholics and Protestants, my mam would get fearful and say to him, "Hush! Not in front of the children!" I know why she was frightened, because so often this business of Catholics and Protestants means that people get killed. Catholic kings and queens kill Protestants, and Protestant rulers kill Catholics.

In 1587 there was much talk about it in the streets and in the wool market at Moorgate, where I worked. The Spanish were expected to invade at any moment and kill all us Protestant English in our beds, including the Queen herself. But for as long as I could remember these same stories had been told, and there had been no sign of any invasion. Although there *had* been attempts on the life of the Queen by Spanish assassins, that I did know. The year before there had been a plot to kill her and it was said that the Queen's own cousin, the Scottish queen, Mary, was involved in it. They had finally executed the traitors by cutting their heads off. Praise be that these assassins have all been defeated and our Queen still lives.

Away from the markets is the rich part of the city, Lombard Street, where the bankers live and work. Uncle Rufus said it is called Lombard Street because most of the bankers came from Lombardy in Italy, way back in the time of King Richard the Lionheart. But my dad said Rufus made things up and would not know the truth if it came up and bit him on the leg. Uncle Rufus is my mam's brother and is a sailor with the famous captain Sir Francis Drake. I used to like it when Uncle Rufus visited because he told exciting stories of his voyages with Captain Drake, but because he knew my dad did not like him, he did not call on us very much.

As I said, when I could I worked on the cloth markets near Moorgate, helping the stall owners when they needed an extra pair of hands. If I was lucky, I sometimes earned as much as two pennies a day, and a penny could buy two good-sized loaves of brown bread, or a pound of beef. We were lucky, with my dad working as a butcher we usually had meat in the house, though not the best cuts. Even a day butcher has to pay for the meat he takes, so Dad usually brought home giblets and offal, which were the cheapest meats to be had. But when stewed, thickened with bread and spiced with pepper he said they tasted as good as many dearer cuts.

One day in February, I was coming home empty-handed. There had been no work for me at Moorgate, nor at any of the other markets. I had walked all over the city looking for work, even going down to the edge of the Thames in case a ferryman should want help with his boat, but I had no luck. I had been lucky with one thing, though. A stallholder I knew had taken pity on me not finding work and had given me half a stale loaf and a piece of cheese, so I had not gone hungry.

By three o' clock it was obvious that there would be no work for me. There was no work to be had after dark and at that time of year night began to fall soon after four.

As I trod the stairs up to our rooms on the first floor of Garlands, I could hear Mam and Dad's voices. Dad was in an angry mood, and Mam was trying to calm him down.

"Please, John—" I heard Mam plead.

But Dad cut her off and snapped, "This is my home, Susan! I pay the rent and I will say what I like. And I say it is time that boy left home to fend for himself! He is an extra mouth we cannot afford to feed!"

"Thomas works and brings money in," my mam protested.

"Not enough for pay for his keep!" replied my dad angrily. "When I was his age I had left my parents for three years!"

"But children are different nowadays," said my mam. "Lots of children are still at home with their parents when they are thirteen."

"At thirteen he should be out earning his own living and looking after himself like I was!" insisted my dad.

I sighed, turned around and walked back down the stairs. I did not fancy going home when Dad was in that kind of mood. I expected he must have had a bad day at the butchery.

I decided to take a walk around the streets for an hour or so and give Dad time to calm down before I returned. Truth be said, my dad was in a bad temper most of the time. Mam said to me once he was like it because we were poor and Dad was worried about finding the money to feed us all. There was never enough money. But all I knew was that other people were poor, and their dads did not complain at them all the time.

Many of the other families at Garlands had no work, or only the little money that they could get from rag-picking and the like. Many of them were little more than beggars, and my dad hated living among them. What he most wanted was a house of our own, but to rent a whole house, however small, cost more money than renting two rooms at Garlands.

I headed for the river. At least there would be something to look at there, watching the boats mooring for the night, furling their sails and dropping anchor. Sometimes people fell into the Thames as they were getting into the small boats, and it was always fun to watch them splashing about.

The Thames was my favourite part of London. I would watch the big ships moored there and imagine going out on one, going to far off lands, seeing exciting new things. Space, that was what I craved. The space of the sea, or the space of the vast new lands that Uncle Rufus told me about. Instead I was stuck here in London, where the houses were tiny and crammed together, and everyone seemed to be living on top of one another. And the smell! Out in the country my cousins had a privy over a hole in the ground, and after they used it they filled it in with earth. We emptied our chamber pots out of our windows, and you were just unlucky if you were underneath it when we did it!

I decided to call on my friend, William Baker. William was 12 and lived with his mother in one room in the basement of a house in a tiny alley not far from the river. Like me, William sometimes worked at the markets. Unlike me, William did not get nagged at to leave home, but then, his money helped to feed both him and his mother.

William was outside his house when I arrived, throwing a ball of rags at the wall and catching it again. His mother had obviously only just cut his hair because it stuck up straight from his head like the bristles of a worn bush.

"Feel like a walk, William?" I asked. "We could go on the Bridge and look at the heads. There will surely be some new ones there after the Scottish Queen had hers cut off."

"They never put the heads of kings and queens on the Bridge, stupid," William pointed out.

"I know, but there were other traitors in the plot and they cut their heads off. Maybe *their* heads will be on spikes."

William nodded in agreement and we began to walk towards London Bridge. From the houses around us came the smells of cooking as people prepared to eat after their day's work. My stomach was empty, and it occurred to me that maybe I should have waited until after we had eaten our supper before I went out for a walk. But then I would have had to face Dad.

As we walked, William turned to me, "Is it true that the Spanish are on their way to invade us?" he asked.

I nodded. "Yes," I said. "That is what everyone says. I can tell even my mam is frightened, though she does not like to talk on it."

"What will you do if they invade, Thomas?" asked William. "Will you fight?"

"Yes," I said. "Mr Petty at the market says if we do not fight they will kill us anyway."

William shook his head and sighed. "I do not understand this business about the war between Catholics and Protestants," he said.

"Nor I neither," I said. "My mam and dad do not like to talk about it, and when I asked Mr Petty what it was about he said 'God and Jesus'. So I asked him did they believe in a different God and Jesus, and he said 'No, 'tis the same one'." I shook my head. "I think it is some kind of madness."

By this time we had reached the river, and we walked along the bank until we came to London Bridge. This was the only way of crossing the river on foot and when you were on it, it was hard to tell it was a bridge, it had so many houses crammed along each side.

At the Southwark end of the bridge was a towered gate, and above the gate's arch the heads of traitors were pinned by iron spikes and left to rot. They were high enough off the ground so that no one could take them off and run away with them, but I had heard of people trying to, often at night. Mostly they were relatives of the traitors who wanted to take the heads and bury them properly.

There were four more new heads on poles since I had last walked here, just three days before, but I did not recognize any of them. Because the heads were so fresh there was quite a crowd gathered on the bridge to look at them and William and I had to push our way through the people to get a proper look. Sir Anthony Babington, who had been part of the plot to put the Scottish Queen on the throne, had been executed some time since and his head was now looking shrunken on its pike, the flesh old and rotting. Like all of the heads before them, the new ones' mouths hung open and their eyes were closed. William and I stood beneath them.

"None of them look like a woman's head," I muttered, disappointed.

Even though I knew that royal heads were never put on display for ordinary people to see, I had hoped that they might put Queen Mary Stuart's head on a pole. After all, she had been found guilty of plotting to kill Queen Elizabeth and have herself put on the throne of England instead, so that made her a traitor.

People like us did not get to see executions where they actually chopped heads off. Only important people, like nobles and royalty were beheaded and we only got to see the ordinary hangings. The gallows nearest to us was at our end of Fetter Lane and sometimes if there was a hanging we would go as a family and watch it. At least, we used to go, but lately Dad did not seem to want to so much. "I do not have time to go to hangings, I have got to go to work and earn money," he would say.

So he would go to work at the butchery and me and Mam and Mary and little Daniel would go along to the gallows and join the crowd.

Most of the hangings were over pretty quickly, although sometimes the hangman would get the weight wrong, or the knot on the noose would slip round to the back of the neck, and the person being hung would not die straight away but would kick and struggle for ages. When that happened, the hangman would have to let them down and then hang them again.

William and I stood in silence looking at the heads for a bit until the crowd became too large and we were being jostled by the people at the back who were impatient to get a better view.

"'Tis time we went before we are trampled underfoot," I muttered.

William and I pushed our way back through the crowd, and then we walked back across the bridge, back to the north side. My quiet manner must have given me away, for William recognized my low humour.

"Is your dad upset with you again?" he asked.

I nodded. "Yes," I sighed. "He wants me to leave home. He thinks I am old enough to look after myself."

"You could always come and stay with me and my mam," suggested William helpfully.

I shook my head.

"No thanks, William, but it is good of you to offer."

William and his mam had a hard life as it was, living in their one room in the basement of a house. It was so near the river that sometimes if the tides were really high their room flooded with water.

"What will you do?" asked William. "You cannot live on the street. They will catch you for vagrancy if you do and you will be whipped and have a hole put in your ear."

"Not yet," I said. "They cannot whip me until I am 14." But it would not be long until I was 14, and I suddenly realized that I would then risk being put in prison, or even hanged!

"My mam will not let my dad put me out in the street," I said, though with more confidence than I felt. "But if he does, and I cannot find anywhere else to live, I will come and stay with you and your mam."

Even living in one damp room was better than being hung from a gallows.

It was getting dark now, and neither William nor I cared to be out on the streets, especially so near the river. Robberies and murders were happening all the time and even though we did not have any money or jewels on us, the robbers could take our clothes, cut our throats, and throw our bodies in the Thames. We did not want to take the chance of being waylaid.

I left William outside his house, and then walked home to Cheapside. When I got up to our rooms I was relieved to find that Dad was asleep on the straw and sacking in the corner of the small room. Mam and Mary were mending clothes in the bigger room and Daniel was with them, playing with a piece of wood. As I walked in Daniel started banging the wood against the floor, as if he was playing a drum. Mam took the stick off him.

"You will wake your father up," she said, "and if you do that he will not be in a good mood."

Then Mam turned to me and asked, "What sort of day did you have today, Thomas?"

I shrugged. "I am afraid I did not get any work," I said. "There was not much business going on so none of the stallholders in the market needed anyone. If I do not have any luck in the market tomorrow I thought I would try the theatre. The plays start tomorrow afternoon, and there might be some rich people who want their horses looked after while they watch them."

Mam sighed. "Do try, Thomas," she urged. "We need all the money we can get with food and clothes to buy."

"I do try, Mam," I said, and gave her a smile, hoping to cheer her up. "There is not a lot of work about. But I do try."

The next morning I was up and about early, even before the sun rose. I wanted to get to the market as the earliest stallholders arrived and get any work there might be. Also I did not fancy having an argument with Dad about my leaving home. I knew I was only putting off the time when we would have a row face to face, but I wanted to get some money together before I left to strike out into the world on my own.

I was lucky. A merchant had arrived with bales of old clothes, and a stallholder paid me to sort them into good clothes and rags. William also found work, mending pots and pans for a tinker. By the time darkness started to fall and the market closed for the day, William and I were able to set off for our homes with money in our pockets. I had earned two pennies, which meant one for me and one for my family. I determined to save my coin, keeping it safe from prying eyes and grabbing hands.

As I went up the stairs to our rooms I heard a

familiar voice bellowing, "And be blowed if this Spaniard did not try and cut my ear off just to get my gold earring off me!"

Uncle Rufus!

He was sitting on the bench in our big room, beside Mam and Mary, with Daniel playing at his feet. Uncle Rufus was a short man with long dark hair that sometimes hung down around his face. This day it was tied at the back of his head like a pony's tail. He also had a beard, trimmed and flecked with grey, against which the gold earring he wore through his left ear shone brightly. As always, his clothes had an ill-fitting look, as if he had borrowed them from someone either two sizes bigger or two sizes smaller. Uncle Rufus cared not much for fashion.

Dad was sitting in his chair, a sullen look on his face. He always looked like this when Mam's brother called.

"Thomas!" beamed Rufus as I came in. "Well well! Look at my nephew! He is getting bigger every time I see him!"

"And hungrier," growled my dad.

Proudly I produced my penny and offered it to him. "Here you are, Dad," I said. "Towards my keep. And with luck there will be another one tomorrow. Mr

Petty at the market says there will be more work for me sorting clothes."

Dad looked at the penny grimly, then gestured towards Mam.

"Give it to your mam," he said. "It is her who buys the food you eat and the clothes you wear."

Mam smiled at me and took the coin. "Thank you, Thomas," she said. "That penny will be most useful."

"Pennies!" laughed Rufus genially. "Why, if you were with Captain Drake you would be earning shillings, boy! You would be a rich man!"

"Like you, eh, Rufus," said my dad pointedly.

"Ah, I am afraid I will never be rich, John," sighed Rufus. "T'aint in my nature. I am a sailor with money. Easy come and easy go. But if I wanted to, if I had saved instead of spent, why, I could buy this house we are in many times over!"

This was too much for Dad. He rose and said, "Well I have to get up early tomorrow to work and earn money to feed my family, so I will bid you goodnight." With that he disappeared into the small room.

Mam cast an anxious look towards Dad, knowing that there would be a terrible row about Rufus once my uncle had gone.

I decided to keep my mouth shut for a while as I did

not want to give Dad even more reason to moan at me. It was a pity because I wanted Uncle Rufus to tell us about his adventures, and he only did this when we asked him. Luckily my sister Mary did the asking instead.

"Did you really sail all the way right round the world, Uncle Rufus?"

"Bless you, yes!" he chortled. "Me and Captain Drake and a handful of brave men. Three years it took us, three years of hardship and adventures the like of which would scare a young lass like you fit to burst!"

It was a story we had all heard before, and often, but one which I loved to hear Uncle Rufus tell over and over. He spoke of faraway countries, of strange people, strange foods, strange animals. Of the whole idea that the world was round instead of flat. Listening to Rufus was a time of wonder. I thought of all the marvellous things that he had seen while travelling, and how my life was confined to these two rooms and the foul-smelling streets of London. There was no adventure here at home, but out there ... out there anything was possible.

That night, after Mam had gone to sleep in the small room with Dad, taking baby Daniel and Mary with her, Uncle Rufus and I settled ourselves down on the floor to sleep. There was only one piece of straw sacking for both of us, but Uncle Rufus insisted I sleep on it.

"I am used to harder floors than this, boy," he said. "I have slept on wooden boards with a cannonball for a pillow. I have slept in mud, and even once on a sleeping crocodile. If you can sleep on a ship that is rolling and tossing in the worst storms you have ever known when you are going through the Roaring Forties, you can sleep anywhere."

I got myself comfortable on my straw pallet, and then I decided to ask the question that had been in my mind the whole time I had sat listening to Rufus talk about his adventures.

"Uncle Rufus," I said, "do you think I could earn a living at sea?"

"You?" he said in surprise. "Why, if anyone could, that person is you, Thomas. A bright strong boy like yourself could make himself rich, believe me. There are spoils out there on the sea, and every man on board ship has a share when we take a prize. There is big money to be made. And any man who can hang on to his money can leave the sea as wealthy as any banker."

"Surely any man can hang on to his money at sea,"

I said. "After all, there is nothing to spend it on."

"There is always something to spend it on, Thomas," said Rufus with a sigh. "When a man gets into port after months at sea, his money soon burns a hole in his breeches pocket. And many a man gambles his money away while he is at sea with cards and dice, so that when he gets his share, 'tis gone before he can leave the ship."

He sighed again, and I knew he was talking about himself and why, for all the tales of riches he spun, he always arrived at our home nearly penniless.

"I should like to earn my living as a sailor," I said.

"A sailor?" chuckled Rufus. "Why, you are a bit young for that yet, young Thomas. But I am sure I could get you on board as a cabin boy. And after that, 'tis up to you."

"A cabin boy would be good," I said earnestly. "Would you have a word for me with Captain Drake? See if he would take me on board his ship?"

There was a short silence while Rufus thought this over, and when he spoke his tone had changed to one more serious. "Are you really sure of this, Thomas? Despite all my tales of the pleasure I get from being out on the ocean with Captain Drake, the truth is that life at sea is hard."

"I am not afraid of hard work, Uncle," I said firmly.

"'Tis not just the hard work," said Rufus. "It looks as if there is a war coming between us and the Spaniards, Thomas, and it appears as if that war is going to be fought on the seas. There will be deaths and injuries, lots of them. I should hate you to be one of them because you had been led astray by my stories."

"Trust me, Uncle," I said. "I am not afraid. I have to make something of my life, and the only way to do that is to take a chance. I could get killed tomorrow by a horse in the street and have done nothing. I need the chance to find my own future, and I want to find out if that future is a life at sea."

In the gloom I saw Rufus's head nod. "Very well," he said. "If you want to go to sea, then I am the man who will get you there. Trust me, Thomas."

The next morning I was awake early and left while Rufus was still fast asleep on the floor. Once again I wanted to get what work there was from Mr Petty before any other boy took it. I also did not want to get caught up in any rows between Dad and my uncle. I prayed that Rufus would remember our talk the night before.

By the time I got home that evening with another two pennies hidden in my stocking, Rufus had gone. I did not tell my mam and dad what he had promised. It was not worth starting another row over something that might not happen. And one thing that Dad said about Rufus was true: he was not very reliable. So I kept my secret to myself and hoped against hope my life at sea would begin soon.

*March 1587*

As February turned into March things continued in the same way. Sometimes I got work and came home with money to give to Mam, sometimes I did not. Dad did not tell me directly to my face that he wanted me to leave, but now and then he would say, "Of course, you are getting to be a man now, Thomas, and you will be wanting to branch out on your own very soon." And then he would ask me what plans I had, and I would say I was thinking about my future and wondering what to do. His reply was always, "Well I would not leave it too long. There are plenty of other young men of your age out there looking for good places. You do not want to lose out because you left it too long."

Once I said to him that I was thinking maybe of going to sea. He just laughed scornfully.

"Sea?" he said. "There is no future at sea! You do not want to listen to the tales your uncle tells, Thomas. Look at him! He is older than me and yet he comes here still without a penny to his name to be fed and housed. You do not want to be doing the same."

After that, I did not say any more about it.

One Sunday morning in March a stranger arrived at our door. He was about 30, though it was hard to tell his age because of the dirt and grime on his face, and most of it was covered with a big bushy beard and long, matted hair.

"Is this the house of John and Susan Hobbs?" he asked.

Mam and Dad looked at the man suspiciously, then at one another, before Dad answered carefully: "It might be. Who asks to know?"

"My name is Stevens," said the man. "I come with a message from your brother, Rufus Clark."

"There is no money in this house!" Dad snapped suspiciously.

The man, Stevens, laughed, and said, looking around, "I can see that for myself."

This only annoyed Dad even more. "Say what your business is and then get you gone," he demanded. "This is a respectable house."

"My business is to collect one Thomas Hobbs and

take him to Dover, where his uncle has got him a berth on board Captain Drake's ship as a cabin boy," replied Stevens.

My mam gave a gasp and put her hand to her mouth, then turned to look at me, her eyes wide. I felt my heart give a leap of joy. Rufus had been as good as his word!

"Thomas?" asked Mam, bewildered. "What is this?"

"By what right is Rufus sending for you?" snapped Dad.

I hesitated, wondering how to put it. Then I plucked up my courage and just let the words come out as calmly as I could. "I am thirteen," I said. "You know I am old enough to leave and make my own way in the world, and I have chosen to go to sea. I asked Uncle Rufus to find me a position, and he has."

At this my mam closed her eyes and bit her knuckles. "Why go to sea now, Thomas?" she begged. "They say there is a war coming! You will be lost to us!"

For a moment I thought she was going to burst into tears, but instead she just stood there, swaying slightly, her eyes closed.

"I will not be lost to anyone," I said. "I will come

home with riches in my pockets, I promise you."

My sister Mary smiled at me, delighted. "My brother going for a sailor!" she laughed. "You will be a hero, just like Uncle Rufus!"

I looked at my dad, who had not said a word, but had gone very white in the face. I could see a mixture of anger and pain in his eyes and in the way he clenched his jaw. Quietly he said, "If that is what you want you had better be gone." And with that he turned and left the house.

Mam opened her eyes as she heard him go. "You should have said something about this before, Thomas," she said in a small voice.

"I am sorry, Mam," I said, "but I did not think it would really happen and I knew Dad would disapprove."

Stevens gave a little cough, and said, "We had better be going sooner rather than later. We have a long way to travel."

I nodded and said, "I will gather my things and be with you after I have said goodbye."

"I will wait for you downstairs," Stevens said, leaving the room.

Mary helped me to put together a bundle containing another jerkin and pair of breeches whilst

Mam found a piece of bread for me to take on the journey.

When I was ready to go, I took the pennies I had saved for myself from the hidey hole I had made in the wall of the big room, and gave them to Mam, all except for one penny which I kept for myself.

"Here, Mam," I said. "This will buy food and clothing for you and Mary and young Daniel."

She looked at the fifteen pennies I held out to her, dumbfounded.

"They are honestly earned," I said. "I have saved them for when I was ready to leave home and start on my own. It seems that time is now."

She shook her head. "You will need them," she said.

"I will not need them where I am going," I told her. "The ship feeds its sailors. I will take one penny for the journey. The rest is yours."

She hesitated, but I thrust the coins at her. "Please," I said. "I need to know you have this money."

Mam hesitated again, then she took the coins from me and put them in her apron. "Thank you, Thomas," she said. And then she threw her arms around me and hugged me close. Mary hugged me, too, and even baby Daniel joined in.

I felt Mam's tears wet on my face and I whispered

to her, "I shall be all right, I promise."

Then I picked up my bundle, and headed for the door. I stopped and gave a last smile to my mam, Mary, and Daniel, and then I left, to set out in the world on my own.

It took us two days to travel from London to Dover. Stevens had arranged transport for us on a cart. He was one of the most silent men I had ever met. He gave no details of himself, nor did he ask any of me. When I volunteered some stories about myself to help pass the time on the journey, Stevens nodded and said simply, "Aye, so I hear from your uncle." So there seemed little point in my carrying on with my tale.

Our whole journey would have passed in complete silence if it had not been for the carter who carried us. He was a merry soul who, I suspect, had had too much ale to drink. Although we all drank ale at home, because the water was too foul to drink and would poison us, I knew never to drink too much else it would addle my wits. The carter was old enough to know not to let drink addle him, but he continued to sup from a leather bottle as we drove along the rutted roads. Between sips, he sang and told us stories about his experiences on the road as a carter. A few times he even fell asleep at the reins and I thought the cart would leave the road and we would be killed or injured, but every time it happened Stevens clambered over on to the driver's seat and took the reins until the carter awoke. The only thing that woke the driver was one of the two horses – or sometimes both – giving a loud and noxious fart, which made him sit up and start waving his hat in front of him to drive away the smell. Then he would break into song again, and we would trundle on our way.

By night we slept in the cart. The carter fell into a deep sleep, full of loud snores, while Stevens and I took turns to keep watch in case thieves tried to steal our belongings. Not that we had much worth stealing, but thieves do not care what they take as long as they think it is easy pickings.

Finally, we arrived at Dover. The carter dropped us just outside the town and Stevens and I walked down to the docks. I could smell the sea in the air, hear the gulls cry and see them whirling overhead. Gulls and water were always to be seen on the Thames, but this was more than just a river, this was the wide, open sea. The home of adventure!

We walked along a narrow cobbled alley, and then suddenly there it was in front of me: our ship, the *Elizabeth Bonaventura*, with its high wooden sides, and its tall masts soaring up into the sky, moored by thick ropes to the dockside.

I expected it to be swarming with men, having heard from Uncle Rufus about the two hundred or so men who served with Drake, but from this distance I could see just a few men on deck, scrubbing the wooden planks. Other men were up on the masts – it was difficult to see what they were doing, but I guessed that they were tying knots in the ropes to repair the rigging.

I followed Stevens up the gangplank, and as my feet touched the wood of the deck, I felt a thrill of pleasure and anticipation run through me. I was going to be a sailor!

"You stay here, I will go and find your uncle," said Stevens.

He went to an open hatch in the deck, walked down some steps, and then vanished into the depths of the ship. Soon I would be going down there too, as a member of the crew. I was standing there dreaming about my new life, when a man's voice spoke just behind me.

"Well, well. What have we here?" he said.

I turned, and came face to face with a short man, very thin in the body, but with enormous gnarled hands at the end of muscular arms. The man gave me a smile, but it was one of the nastiest smiles I had ever seen. I backed away from him, but found myself pressed against a large wooden box fixed to the deck.

"You the new cabin boy?" he asked.

"Yes," I said. Then I gulped, and added, "And I am not afraid of you."

The man's smile broadened. "Ain't you, though," he chuckled. "You will be soon enough, boy. You see, this is going to be a long voyage, and I need a willing slave to look after me. Seems to me as I will get in first and lay my claim to you before anyone else does."

The man leered at me and grabbed me by the arm. I was just getting ready to give him a hard kick on the shins, when a fist came out of nowhere and thumped him in the side of the head. The man stumbled and fell down on to the deck. Then he pulled a knife from his belt and turned to face his attacker. It was Uncle Rufus.

"Better put that knife away, Simnel, afore I take it off you and cut your ears off," growled Rufus.

Simnel hesitated, wondering whether it was worth

going for Rufus with the knife, but then Rufus produced a short length of chain from behind his back.

"I said put it away, Simnel, or so help me I will wrap this round your throat and you will be feeding the fishes."

Simnel scowled, but pushed his knife back into the sheath in his belt.

"And if you lay one finger more on my nephew here, you will have me to answer to," added Rufus. "Remember that."

Simnel looked at me, surprised. "Your nephew?" he said. And then he laughed, trying to make a joke of it. "If I had known he was your nephew I would not have tried my little joke on him." Turning to me, he grinned and said, "Just my bit of fun. We do it to all the new boys. No harm done, eh?"

But I did not smile back at him. I knew he was just making light of it for my uncle's sake. "I do not like that sort of fun," I said sharply.

Simnel hesitated and then forced a laugh. "He is a proud one, Rufus, and no mistake," he chuckled, but there was no good humour in his laugh.

Rufus watched Simnel go, then he turned to me. "I am sorry about that, Thomas," he said.

"That's all right, Uncle," I said. "I was just about to

give him a good kick when you arrived."

"That one needs more than a good kick," nodded Rufus soberly. "He is new to this crew this time out. Captain Fenner has had a hard time finding men for this voyage, so he has taken what he can. Some are brought from prisons, some are pressganged. Where Simnel comes from, I do not know. All I say is, stay away from him as much as you can." Then he grinned and slapped me heartily on the shoulder. "Anyway, Thomas, forget that scum. Follow me and I will show you to your quarters."

We headed for the open hatch I had seen Stevens step into earlier. Some wooden stairs took us "below decks", taking us past the top deck where Rufus told me the officers lived, to the gundeck below.

"This is it," said Rufus. "Your home for this voyage."

The gundeck was the whole width of the ship, with cannons fixed to their positions along the sides by thick ropes. Beside each cannon was a wooden box filled with cannonballs. The ceiling was just about a foot above my head, barely about six feet high. Any man who was tall would have to walk around bent over to avoid banging his head against the roof beams.

A few wooden chests were pushed against the outer

walls of the ship, but there was no sign of any beds.

"Where do I sleep?" I asked.

"On the wood floor, along with the rest of us," said Rufus. " 'Tis hard at first, but you will get used to it." He chuckled. "We used to have straw to sleep on at night, but after it caught fire on some ships, the Admirals of the Fleet banned it. Mind, it is all right for them admirals and captains and the like, they have proper bunks to sleep in."

"There do not seem to be many men for a ship this big," I commented.

"This ain't the proper crew," said Rufus. "We are the crew to get the ship ready and take her along the coast to Plymouth, where the rest of the men come aboard. Tomorrow our captain, Captain Fenner, will be arriving, and shortly after he joins us I expect that we will be setting sail for Plymouth. Anyways, I had better show you over the ship, where things are and what you have to do, that sort of thing. So follow me, but be sure not to touch anything unless I say you can. This here ship has already been cleaned from top to bottom and back again, and I do not want my nephew messing it up and getting me into trouble now, do I?"

With that, Uncle Rufus began a tour of the ship, pointing out the various parts and telling me their proper names. I learnt that the left side at sea was called the port side, and what on land we called the right was called starboard. The bow was the front of the ship and aft was the back. I learnt about the fo'c'sle – which was where the officers were stationed at the front of the ship – and the bulwarks and much more. By the end of it my head was spinning.

"Do not worry," grinned Rufus. "It took me nigh on five years at sea to learn all them words and what they mean. Do not expect to remember everything at once."

One thing had puzzled me. In the whole tour I had not once seen a privy. When I asked Uncle Rufus he laughed out loud.

"Privy?" he chortled. "Why, nephew, there is no such thing as a privy on board a boat. Instead 'tis expected that when you want to pee you do so in a bucket and pour it into one of them big open barrels you can see on the deck. That is very important because it comes in very handy if there is ever a fire on board the boat while we are at sea. And if you want to do more than just have a pee, then follow me and find out how you go about it."

With a broad grin, Rufus strode along the deck towards the bow, and I followed. As we walked I saw the figure of Simnel lurking in the shade of the mast, and I knew that his eyes were on us, watching with a venomous look.

At the bow of the ship, on either side, sticking out over the sea was a series of long planks, every one with a series of holes in it, each hole just big enough for a man to sit in.

"Here we are," chuckled Rufus. "This is called the 'necessary seat'. That is where you sit when you want to do the necessary. It is all clean now, but I tell you it will be a different matter when we hit high seas and the boat is a-rolling and a-rocking from side to side. The bow of the ship gets plastered on both sides. In high summer, if the sun is hot, by my nose it smells something strong! That is when we need the high seas so the waves can clean the muck off."

I imagined trying to sit on one of those planks while a storm raged and waves smashed against the bow of the ship, and wondered how many people had been swept to their death at sea while emptying their bowels. The very thought of it made mine tremble.

That first night, as darkness fell, I stood with Uncle Rufus and Stevens and looked out across the sea, listening to the waves lapping against the side of the hull.

"Out in the dark over there across that sea, that is France, Thomas," said Rufus, pointing out into the inky blackness. "And beyond that is Spain. And that is where we are bound for this time, from what I heard Mr Berry, the Master, tell the purser. Though I expect we must wait till Captain Drake himself comes on board and gives us our orders."

The thought of seeing the famous Captain Francis Drake himself coming on board this ship made me quake with excitement.

"Captain Drake will be on this ship?" I asked. "I thought you said Captain Fenner was the captain."

"Captain Fenner is in charge," nodded Rufus. "But this here is not just any old ship, the *Elizabeth Bonaventura* is Drake's flagship. That means Drake himself stays aboard her. This is the most important ship in the fleet, my boy. You are honoured to be serving aboard it."

I was puzzled. "Then if Captain Drake will be aboard here, and Captain Fenner, why is Mr Berry called the Master? Is not the Master the one who is in charge?"

Stevens laughed. "Nay," he said. "Being the Master means he is in charge of navigating the ship."

And then Uncle Rufus and Stevens explained to me

who was who when it came to running the ship. It seemed that as cabin boy everyone on board ship could give me orders and I had to obey them. But some people's orders were more important than others. The most important person was Drake himself, followed by Captain Fenner, the captain of the *Bonaventura*. There was some argument between Rufus and Stevens over this, with Stevens saying that in his book Mr Nichols, Drake's own chaplain, was just as important as Captain Fenner. He said that Drake was a God-fearing man so he took just as much advice from Mr Nichols as he did from Captain Fenner.

As the Master, Mr Berry was next one down from Captain Fenner. It was his eye watching the sea and the skies to make sure we did not hit rocks or run into whirlpools or bad seas. Under him he had four quartermasters, each one in charge of a separate quarter of the ship.

Next came the boatswain or "bosun", Mr Pugh. He was in charge of the sails, the tackle, twine, the sailcloth, everything to do with how the ship was rigged. He was also responsible for making sure the ship was ready when it came time for action, making sure the ballast and cargo were stowed well away and secure and not in the way of the guns.

Mr Harris, the carpenter, was in charge of all repairs to the boat. Rufus and Stevens told me that many a boat had been saved from sinking at sea by the skills of the ship's carpenter. Mr Belson, the master gunner, was in charge of all the guns on board and had to know the distance and power of each gun. He had four quarter gunners under him, each responsible for a quarter of the ship's guns.

Also there was the purser, who kept all the records of the money that the men earned, and owed; the ship's surgeon; and the coxswain, who was in charge of the longboats. Below all these came the mates: the bosun's mate and the coxswain's mate. Then there were the stewards, and the cook and his men. All in all, there would be a lot of men on board to give me orders and keep me busy.

That night I laid myself down on some sacking spread on the lower deck, next to Uncle Rufus, surrounded by the rest of the crew, save those who were up on deck keeping watch. As I lay there, listening to the snoring of the sailors and smelling the wood of the ship and the sea, I thought I would be too excited to sleep. But what with the rocking of the ship on the water, coupled with the business of the day, I soon felt drowsy, and before I knew it I fell into a deep sleep.

The next morning, as Rufus had predicted, Captain Fenner came on board. He was a tall, serious-looking man, with a frown on his face as if he was thinking about a problem. I thought he might be worried about something to do with the ship, but Rufus told me that was how Captain Fenner always looked, it was just his nature.

The next few days I was set to work, cleaning and scrubbing the decks, and then hanging over the side on rope netting and cleaning the side of the boat. Rufus said the boat had to be clean at the start of a voyage to stop disease from coming on board. I noticed that I was the only boy in the crew, and asked Rufus if I was to be the only servant of everyone on board. Rufus laughed and said that more boys would be joining the ship later when it took on its full crew.

"But there will be no time for games with other young boys, Thomas," he said affectionately. "Once we set to sea, 'twill be work, work, work. Trust me."

I had noticed that Simnel was staying away from

me. But I could tell from the way he looked at me sideways that he bore a grudge and wanted vengeance. I expect it was because my uncle had threatened him and made him back down in front of me, but I swore to myself that I would take no chances while Simnel was around. I felt he would as likely slip a knife in my back as look at me.

On 26th March the great man himself, Captain Sir Francis Drake, came aboard the *Elizabeth Bonaventura* and took command. As he came up the gangplank on to the ship, Uncle Rufus made sure that he was standing near the end of the gangway, with me standing next to him.

"Captain, sir!" said Rufus, and he threw in a smart salute.

"Good morrow to you, Rufus Clark!" nodded Drake. "I am glad to see you have rejoined us!"

"May I never go to sea again if I fail to journey with Captain Drake," said Rufus. "I have brought my nephew, Thomas, for to be a cabin boy on this trip."

"A new cabin boy, eh?" said Drake. "Good. Where is he?"

Rufus thrust me forward. "Here, sir!" he said.

I stood as stiffly to attention as I could, hoping to impress the great Sir Francis Drake. He was shorter than I expected, with a thick bushy crop of red hair sprouting from his head and hanging down around his ears, and a neatly trimmed pointed beard, also red. Drake looked at me and nodded approvingly.

"He holds himself well," Drake said to Rufus. "How do you do, boy? Do you know who I am?"

I nodded.

"Cat got your tongue?" he asked.

"No, sir," I said. "I was afraid to speak without being asked to."

Drake nodded approvingly. "A boy who knows his place," he said. "That is what we need on this voyage. Someone who is ready to obey orders. Is that you?"

"That is me, sir!" I said fervently.

"Good," nodded Drake.

Then I spotted another man walking up the gangplank. He was dressed all in black from head to foot, and with a face so set and white and angry-looking that I thought at first he must be a hangman.

"Ah, Mr Nichols!" boomed Drake heartily. "Come and meet our latest crew member. Young Thomas, our new cabin boy!"

Mr Nichols looked at me, unsmiling. Then, to my shock, he thrust his face close to mine and demanded, "Do you hate Catholics, boy?"

I was startled at the suddenness of the question. Did *I* hate Catholics? I knew my dad did, and Mr Petty, and so I supposed I must do, too. But the real truth was I did not even know any Catholics, so I did not really know if I would hate them! Behind Nichols's back I saw Uncle Rufus frantically mouthing "Yes" at me silently, and I stammered out, "Y–yes."

Mr Nichols nodded, satisfied. "Good," he said. "Then you shall have much pleasure on this journey. We shall attack them and damn their souls to hell!"

Drake slapped the man on the shoulder. "Well said, Philip!" he exclaimed cheerfully. "Now, let us go below and converse with Captain Fenner. We have much to plan."

I watched them go, admiring the great Sir Francis Drake, and the confident way he walked. He had the same slight roll that I noticed Uncle Rufus and Stevens had, which came, I supposed, from spending most of their lives at sea on a ship that never stayed still and flat.

"There," Rufus said proudly when Captain Drake and Mr Nichols had gone below. "Now you have met the man. Is not the Captain everything as fine as I said he would be?"

"Indeed he is," I agreed, but I could not say the same thing about his chaplain, Mr Nichols. There had been an intensity in his eyes when he questioned me that was similar to the venomous look in Simnel's when I first came on board.

I did not have much time to dwell further on this, because a few minutes after Captain Drake was aboard, there came a call from the bosun's mate which echoed across the decks: "Prepare the rigging. Check the sails. We sail at first light on the morning tide!"

So the next morning, 27th March, I began my first journey at sea. Even though Uncle Rufus and Stevens said the sea was calm, to me it felt as if I was riding on board a cart that had two broken wheels on one side. The *Bonaventura* rocked in the waves, riding up and then crashing down. I found it hard to walk without falling over and when I moved I had to find something to hang on to. Rufus and Stevens thought this very funny.

"Wait tell you get out to sea proper, Thomas," laughed Rufus.

"Aye," grinned Stevens. "Can you imagine how young Thomas would be out in the high seas?" And they both laughed out loud.

"Out there we will have waves that are fifty ... nay, a hundred feet high, that toss a ship about as if it was no more than a feather," explained Rufus. "I have seen a whole ship just disappear beneath one wave, not even the mast coming back up." He gestured out at the sea around us dismissively. "This is a calm sea, Thomas. Believe me, when you get into rough sea, you will know it."

It may not have been rough as far as Rufus was concerned, but it was enough to make me feel sick. After an hour I could feel the contents of my stomach rising, and I just managed to struggle across to the rail around the boat in time. Unfortunately for me, just as I reached it the boat gave a lurch and the wind blew and threw the puke back at me, all over the front of my shirt and breeches. I felt such shame! It was bad enough that I had been sick, but to do so all over myself was a terrible humiliation.

I was heading below to change my clothes, when Simnel appeared and grinned at me.

"Well, 'tis the cabin boy!" he said. "And it looks like he has not got the stomach for shipboard life. Or if he has, his stomach seems to be all over his clothes."

"Not for much longer," I said, and I went to push

past him, but he held on to me.

"Nay," he said. "Do you not know it is a punishable offence to change your clothes once we have set sail?"

I tried to disentangle his fingers from my shirt collar, but the grip of his fingers was like iron.

"Let me go," I said. "I will deal with you when I have changed my clothes!"

"What is going on?" snapped a voice.

Simnel and I both looked round. It was Stevens.

"This whelp was going below to change his dirty clothing," said Simnel. "Lucky I stopped him afore he got into trouble. Maybe you will tell his uncle what a good friend I have been to the boy."

With that Simnel gave me a smile, and went on his way, laughing out loud.

I looked at Stevens, puzzled by the concerned expression on his face.

"What did he mean?" I asked.

"What Simnel says is true," said Stevens. "It is the rules. No change of clothes once a voyage has begun. You can wash the ones you have, but it is better not to wear wet clothes unless you have to. Let the puke dry and then you can scrape it off, 'tis better."

I looked at him, stunned. "You are not serious in this?" I asked.

"It is the rule on board ship," Stevens nodded. He gave me a friendly smile. "You will find there are many rules, Thomas, and it is best to keep them if you do not want to fall foul of the Captain."

*April 1587*

It took us three days of sailing to get to Plymouth, along the south coast of England. For the whole journey we kept near enough to the coast to keep it in sight, though far enough away to keep clear of rocks and sandbanks. Just off the Isle of Wight we were joined by some merchant ships that Rufus said were owned by friends of Captain Drake.

"They will help us carry the prizes we will bring back with us from Spain," he explained.

"Plunder," grinned Stevens, and he licked his lips in anticipation.

At Plymouth I expected the crew to swarm on board, but there was only a handful of men waiting for us when we tied up at the dock.

I was coiling a rope on deck and I heard Captain Drake and Captain Fenner questioning the man who brought the new crew aboard, a man called Rook.

"Is this all?" demanded Drake angrily. "The *Bonaventura* needs 250 mariners and 30 gunners. And we need soldiers! This rabble is barely enough crew to man a longboat!"

"The men in Plymouth seem wary of coming on this voyage, Captain Drake," said Rook awkwardly. "There are rumours that there may be battles on land when the fleet reaches Spain, and some men say they are sailors not soldiers."

"They will be whatever I tell them to be!" snapped Drake, and his face flushed red with anger, almost matching his hair and beard. "They are cowardly rats and I will have them on board, for in two days we sail! Take a pressgang and bring them in!"

Rook hesitated, then he said, "I fear that many of the men have already left Plymouth."

"Then I will put out a warrant and have them arrested and hanged for desertion and treason!"

"That will still leave us with less than a full crew," pointed out Captain Fenner.

Drake nodded. "That is true," he agreed. "Rook, take a gang and bring as many men as you can. Promise them good wages when this campaign is done. Those you cannot bring by promises, press them and bring them, because we sail at high water on the 2nd of April, the Devil or no!"

Rook left the ship promptly with a party of tough-looking men to find crew.

I had seen pressgangs at work in London. Their job was to find sailors for ships, and they used many ways to do it. One was simply offering a man a job on board ship, but many men would not take them, knowing that it would mean many months at sea, with no way of leaving the ship if they did not like life aboard. So, if men could not be persuaded to come aboard willingly, and if a ship was in desperate need of crew, a pressgang often brought them against their will, sometimes filling them with enough drink to make them drunk and bringing them aboard ship to sober up. If that failed, then some men were simply kidnapped, brought on board ship and held as prisoners in the hold until the ship was at sea, when they were released to work. On a few occasions back home in London I had seen men come staggering drunkenly out of a tavern to be set upon by a gang, and then taken off and carried on to a ship.

By now the *Elizabeth Bonaventura* was just one ship in a large fleet. At 550 tons, she was the largest, but anchored near us in the harbour were others of almost equal size: the *Golden Lion*, *Rainbow*, *Dreadnaught*, as well as the smaller *Spy* and *Cygnet*. Further out in the bay there was a mixture of ships large and small. The talk among the crew was that this great fleet was being assembled for the raid on Spain.

"Look at 'em, boy! 'Tis a fleet to gladden the heart of any Englishman!" Rufus said to me as we stood by the rail and looked out at the gathering of ships. "I know them all! Those there are the warships *Drake*, *Thomas*, *Elizabeth*, *White Lion*, and *Hawkins*. And see there, those are the merchant ships that will be sailing with us: the *Minion*, *Merchant Royal*, *Susan* and *Edward Bonaventura*."

"But when will we sail, Uncle?" I asked.

Rufus sighed. "When the Captain can get a crew. Trouble is, Thomas, I bet my boots that every ship in the fleet is also looking for a crew at the same time. And, despite what the Captain says, a ship cannot put to sea without a proper crew."

Over the next two days Rook and his men searched the streets and inns of Plymouth. Sailors and armed soldiers were among those they brought back, but some were the meanest-looking villains I had ever laid eyes on. I overheard Stevens say to Rufus, as yet another bunch of men came aboard, "When we get to fight the Spaniards we should be as careful to keep our eyes in the backs of our heads, Rufus. These men would slit our throats to increase their share of the plunder."

Among the new crew was a boy who looked a bit younger than me. I had already spotted Simnel, working up in the rigging, making sure that he saw each new arrival from his high perch, like a vulture on the lookout for carrion. As the new boy came up the gangplank, I decided to step in and warn him about Simnel.

"Welcome aboard," I greeted the boy. "My name is Thomas and I am a cabin boy on board. What is your name?"

The boy looked at me, and sneered. "My name is my own business," he said. "And I will trouble you to stay out of it."

With that he swept past me with the rest of the men, leaving me feeling angry and humiliated. Very well, then, I thought, let Simnel have you and be damned to you.

I soon forgot about his insolence as the new crew were assigned their work and their stations, and we worked frantically to prepare our ship for the long voyage to Spain.

One afternoon Mr Pugh, the bosun, ordered me up the rigging to take some needles aloft to a sailor who was fixing a sail to a spar. When I looked up I felt as if my stomach had shrunk. The sailor looked so high up, and the ropes I had to climb looked so frail that I feared I would not be able to do so.

"Go on, lad," said Mr Pugh. "Let us see if you can do it. And how quickly you can do it. We will need monkeys for climbing the ropes when we are out against the Spaniards."

I put the packet of needles in the pocket of my breeches, took hold of the rope netting, and began my climb up. The first few pulls up were easy, but then the ropes began to move left and right as I climbed, and I had to grip tight with every step so as not to slip off them. Higher and higher I went. Rufus and Stevens had told me the trick to climbing the rigging was not to look down, but I could not resist a glance down to see how high I had come. As soon as I looked, I wished I had not. Far below me was the deck, and the men moving around like ants. Suddenly the ship lurched as a wave hit it broadside on. It was only a small wave, and down at deck level I would barely have felt it, but up here even the slightest movement sent the whole topmast lurching many feet one way, and then many feet back the other.

*Keep going*, I murmured to myself as I clung on to the ropes. *Courage. Keep going.*

I turned my gaze back up the rigging, and started climbing again until I had reached the man waiting for the needles. When I did he grinned as he took the packet from me.

"Well done, younker!" he said. "We will make a sailor of you yet!"

And when I dropped back down on to the deck after my return journey, Mr Pugh gave me an approving look. "Good boy," was all he said, but for a man of few words like Mr Pugh, that was praise indeed.

As I walked away from him, I saw the new boy looking me at me. He turned away, but not before I had seen the scowl on his face. For some reason I appeared to have made an enemy of him, but for the life of me I could not think why.

On the morning of 2nd April the whole crew of the *Elizabeth Bonaventura* were assembled on the main deck. Looking down on us from the rail that edged the fo'c'sle were Captain Drake, Captain Fenner, and the Chaplain, Mr Nichols.

"Lads," announced Drake in ringing tones, his West Country accent stronger than ever, "we are about to embark on a great adventure. You all know Philip, King of Spain, to be a villain who has plotted to kill our dear Queen Elizabeth and place himself on the throne of England. So far, thanks to good intelligence and the bravery of her subjects, all these attempts have failed. But now this Spanish peacock has the audacity to try and do by sea what he has so far failed to do on land. Yes, lads, he plans to set sail an Armada of warships from Spain to invade our beloved country! To send Spanish boots striding over England's soil! Well he will not do it as long as Francis Drake is alive! And I trust the same goes for you! What say you?"

"I say we are with you, Captain Drake, every man jack of us, or some of us will know the reason why!" roared a voice, and I turned and saw that it was Uncle Rufus who had shouted.

"Well spoken, Rufus Clark!" said Drake, and on hearing Drake say my uncle's name so fondly among so many, I felt a swelling of pride in my chest. "There speaks a man who has sailed with me for many a long year and on many a voyage. You heed his words, lads. He is one of your own and you can trust him!"

"Like I would trust a snake," whispered a voice in my ear. I knew without looking round that it was Simnel.

Drake continued addressing the crew. "We are going to stop the Spaniard even before he begins. Today we sail for Cadiz, where our intelligence says the Spanish fleet is being gathered, and there we will burn every ship." Then he smiled broadly and added, "But not before we have plundered them and taken every doubloon, every piece of gold and jewellery, every thing of value that we can. And if there is not enough treasure for us on those Spanish ships, then by Heaven we shall take what treasure there is in the town itself."

This was what the crew wanted to hear and they cheered loudly. Saving England was all very well, but money and treasure made the prospect of victory sweeter.

Drake gestured with his hand for silence, and the cheering died down.

"When we face the Spanish, let no man shirk his duty. Remember, if we fail, then England will be lost. Our Queen Elizabeth will be lost. And if the Spanish set foot on England's soil, then your families and everything you hold dear will be lost. Let us pray."

We all closed our eyes and bowed our heads, and then I heard the voice of Mr Nichols, harsh and angry: "Lord, in the coming struggle give us victory against the evil forces of the Pope. May the King of Spain and his Catholic accomplices burn in Hell and suffer damnation and fire and brimstone for ever."

And he went on in this way for a good ten minutes, his voice getting louder and ever more strident.

After, as we dispersed to our stations, I said to Rufus: "Mr Nichols hates Catholics worse than anyone I have ever known. Why?"

Rufus hesitated, and then said, "'Tis a long story. Too long for now when we have the ship to make ready for sail. I will tell you when we both have time on our passage to Spain. Now, 'tis time to get to your station. This ship will not sail on its own."

Once we were clear of the coast, I began to see what Rufus and Stevens had meant about the high seas. They may not have been waves 50- or 100-feet high, but they were big enough to make the *Elizabeth*

*Bonaventura* roll and rock from side to side. I did my best to learn how to move with the ship as I walked across the deck, whilst at the same time trying to ignore my heaving stomach.

That first night out on the open sea I felt proud of myself. As I headed for the gundeck and my bed – if you could call a hard piece of bare board a bed – I told myself that I had now climbed the rigging, and lasted one full day out on the high sea without puking. I was a sailor!

Passing a pile of ropes coiled in great bundles, I heard a snuffling sound, which made me stop. Cautiously I peered round the coils and found the new boy crouching down and crying softly. For a second I did not know what to do. This was the boy who had dismissed me with a sneer when he came on board so my first reaction was to feel little sympathy for him. But then I remembered what my mam had once told me about people: even the hardest has a soft side, and often the harder they appear, the softer they are.

"Are you unwell?" I asked gently.

The boy stopped sniffling and stood up and glared at me, wiping the tears from his eyes with an angry gesture. "Nay!" he said, anger in his voice. "And I need no help from you!"

With that he slipped out from behind the coils of rope and hurried off to the gundeck and his bed. I shrugged and followed him below to my own. If that was the way he felt, so be it.

On my second night out at sea, I decided to ask Rufus why Mr Nichols hated Catholics so.

Rufus looked around to make sure that no one was within earshot, and then he began to talk in a low voice. "Religion is a hard thing, Thomas," he said. "I am just a simple sailor and all I know of it is what the preacher reads to me from the Bible at service. I *do* know that in my own lifetime religion has brought death and misery to hundreds of people, though 'tis best not to say that out loud because there are many who would have someone killed for expressing their views on the matter."

"I will not tell anyone that you said anything to me," I promised. "Cross my heart and hope to die if I should ever tell. But I wish to understand what all this talk is of Catholics and Protestants. My dad says we are Protestants and the enemies of England are Catholics. But he also says that the last Queen of

England was a Catholic. How is this so?"

Rufus nodded, thinking it over, and then started to explain. "Long before you were born, Thomas, when our Queen's father, King Henry, was on the throne, he wanted a new queen. One who would give him a son and heir. But the Pope in Rome would not allow him to divorce his queen and take a new wife. So Henry says 'I am king of this country, not the Pope. I shall divorce her and do whatever I want.' But the Pope excommunicated him, which meant that Henry could no longer be in the Catholic church. So Henry said, 'A fig to that, I shall be my own church!' At the same time there were lots of others who also wanted to break from the Church of Rome, and they did. The Pope, of course, said that everyone who refused his authority was to be burned at the stake as a heretic."

"Now when Henry died his son, Edward, became king. Not for long, because he died young, nigh as young as you are today. So Henry's eldest daughter Mary became queen. And Mary was the most fanatical Catholic you ever did hear of, and she ordered everyone in England to be Catholic again and follow the Pope on pain of death. So we all did. I was just a young lad of five years old and your mother was just four, so it did not matter to me whether I was

Catholic or Protestant, just so long as I had food in my belly and clothes on my back. But many people said they did not want to be under the Pope, and so Mary was as good as her word and she had those who refused to become Catholics killed, most of them burnt at the stake."

"Mary was only queen for five years, and when she died, Elizabeth, who was her sister, became queen. Now, except in the way of being obstinate, Elizabeth was as different from Mary as chalk is from cheese, and she said she was going back to her father's religion, which was the new Church of England. And so she did. Only this time there were many people left who had been in power with Mary who were devout Catholics and they said they would die before they gave up their religion. So Elizabeth gave them their wish."

"She killed them?" I said, awed.

Rufus nodded. "Same as her sister killed Protestants, Elizabeth killed Catholics. Though not so many as Mary had. Anyways, the Pope was really angry at what Elizabeth did because it meant he had lost England again from his Holy Catholic Empire. So he put a price on her head, promising thousands of gold coins to anyone who killed her. His plan was to put her cousin Mary, the Scottish queen, who was a staunch Catholic, on the throne in her place."

"But Elizabeth had the Scottish Mary's head cut off," I said, knowledgeably. "I went down to London Bridge to see if it was there, but it was not."

"Well, that was the last straw for the Pope," said Rufus. "He and the Spanish King Philip have decided that if England will not become Catholic one way, they will make it become Catholic another. By force."

"But that still does not answer why Captain Drake and Mr Nichols are so against Catholics," I said.

Rufus looked around, then lowered his voice even more and whispered: "Captain Drake's family were fierce Protestants when Queen Mary was alive. They suffered under her, and he has never forgiven that. I expect it is the same with Mr Nichols. But one word of warning, Thomas. Remember, we ordinary people are not supposed to even think about such things. Plus there are spies everywhere, both Catholic and Protestant. A word in the wrong ear, a wrong look, and you could very easily end up with your throat cut. That is why I keep my mouth shut about it. Like I said, terrible things are done in the name of religion."

Until our ship was far out to sea, with no land in any direction, it had never occurred to me just how vast the oceans were. The *Bonaventura*, which seemed so huge when tied up by a wharf, appeared so small in the ocean, especially when the waves rose and hurled the vessel about. We were at sea for three days before we saw land again, at Cape Finisterre, on the north-west coast of Spain. As the shout of "Land ahoy" came down from the crow's nest high up on the mast, I joined with the others in hurrying to the rail to get my first glimpse of a foreign land. On the horizon I could just make out rocks jutting out of the sea, and beyond them, a coastline. It was the country of the enemy, and we were heading straight towards it.

As we neared Cape Finisterre a storm blew up and our ship was tossed about like a cork for another four days, before the storm settled down and we were finally able to head south. On 16th April our fleet arrived just outside Lisbon harbour, far enough away from the coast to be outside the range of the Portuguese cannons, but near enough to see the masts of the ships in the harbour.

"Any bets the Captain goes into Lisbon and plunders the Portuguese?" Stevens asked Rufus.

Rufus shook his head. "Nay," he said. "My money

says we sail on to Cadiz and attack the Spanish fleet. 'Tis not just the treasure the Captain is after on this trip. He intends to stop the Spaniards from invading England. That is what he says, and I have sailed long enough with Captain Drake to know that what he says, he means."

Exactly as Uncle Rufus had forecast, we sailed on south, leading the rest of the fleet down to Cape St Vincent, and then due east towards Cadiz.

I could not help but be frightened of what lay ahead of us. Here we were, seventeen fighting ships, with Drake's flagship at the head of the fleet, close enough to the Spanish and Portuguese coasts to have been seen many times over. Why did the Spanish not send out their warships to attack us? It was true that none of our ships were flying any sort of flag that might identify us as English, but surely this many ships sailing together, especially with things as they were between England and Spain, had to be suspicious. I wondered if they were waiting until we got to Cadiz, where they would mount an ambush against us.

One night, as Stevens and I were sharing watch, keeping observation for any sign of the enemy, I asked him why the Spanish seemed to be doing nothing and if he thought it was part of a trap they were leading us into.

"Could be," said Stevens. "Though if you ask me, it is more likely the Spanish are afeared of coming out and fighting Captain Drake on the open seas because they know what has happened afore. There is no one as good as Captain Drake for handling a ship at sea. As for them setting a trap for us, they tried that before and failed. The truth is, Thomas, they do not know what Captain Drake is going to do next, so all they can do is sit and wait. They know full well that they might set a trap with thousands of men in Cadiz to protect the Spanish fleet moored there, but Drake may go on to attack ships in another harbour. He has done it afore. They will not know what he is thinking or planning," Stevens chuckled. "To be honest, Thomas, I am not sure the Captain knows sometimes what he is planning, he just sort of does it. That is why he is a very difficult enemy to fight."

On the morning of 19th April our fleet arrived just off the coast of Cadiz, and we all anchored our position. I watched as longboats were lowered from each of the other ships, and men climbed down the rigging into them. One by one each longboat set out towards us, the oars of the rowers dipping into the waves and pushing each tiny boat forward.

"Captain Drake's Conference," said Rufus, who had joined me at the rail to watch the boats.

"Conference?" I asked.

"Afore Captain Drake launches an attack he brings all his captains on board his ship to tell them what they are to do as their part of his whole plan. He calls it his Conference. He will have his plan all ready, I can tell you, and he will expect his captains to stick to his orders. Captain Drake is a man who cannot abide men who disobey his orders." Looking out again at the approaching longboats, he added quietly, "I was there when he had a captain executed for disobeying him."

I looked at Rufus, shocked. "He had a captain executed?" I echoed.

"Ssssh!" said Rufus sharply. " 'Twas a long time ago, but best not to talk about it. I only tell you so you will know that this will not be a long Conference, with points for and against the attack being argued. This is just for giving his orders. We will not have to wait long afore we are in action."

I decided that while we were at anchor I would go back below decks and see if I could not get a few minutes' rest before the action started. I was fairly sure that once we went into battle there would be no time for rest of any sort, let alone a chance for sleep.

As I was going down the stairs, I heard a man's voice, harsh and grating and a boy crying out fearfully, "No! Please, no!" I hurried down the stairs, and saw Simnel's back. He was in an alcove holding the new boy by the collar with one hand, while slapping him hard around the face with the other.

"You do not like it, boy, do you? Then maybe you had better do as I say in future and make me feel nicer towards you!" said Simnel.

Forgetting for a moment that I was afraid of Simnel myself, I launched myself at his back and grabbed him by the hair, pulling his head back. Simnel bellowed and lashed out wildly behind him, his great fist knocking me down on to the wooden deck. As I scrambled to my feet I saw that he had let the boy go and was now advancing on me.

"Touch me with one finger and my uncle will kill you!" I warned, doing my best not to let him see that I was quaking inside.

"If I kill you, your uncle will not even know about it," snarled Simnel. "No one will. Your body will just disappear over the side."

"Then you had better be quick about it," I said,

speaking sharply, desperate to stop those huge hands and gnarled fingers from taking hold of me. "For he is on his way down here now. He just sent me on ahead."

Simnel stopped and looked at me, trying to work out if I was lying. "This will keep for later," he snarled, deciding I might be telling the truth after all. "Till then, one word of this to your uncle, and your little friend here will suffer as he has never suffered before. Is that clear?" With that, Simnel pushed me roughly aside and stamped angrily up the stairs.

I went to the boy, who was still shaking. "It is all right, he has gone," I told him.

The boy was looking at me in disbelief. "Why did you attack him?" he asked. "He could have killed you."

"He could have, but he did not," I said, and I told him about my first encounter with Simnel, and how Rufus had saved me.

The boy lowered his eyes. "I am sorry for the way I was with you before," he said. "I was warned not to get too friendly on ships but to keep myself to myself."

"Let me tell my uncle what he has been doing to you," I said. "Rufus will stop him from doing it again."

"No!" said the boy desperately, and in fear. "You heard what he said! If you tell your uncle, Simnel will make me suffer."

"That is the way bullies thrive," I said. "Uncle Rufus says that fear is their hold over you. He says that if you tell others about what they do, you take that fear and their hold over you away."

The boy shook his head. "No," he said. "I will deal with Simnel in my own way. Please, for the moment, do not say what you saw. Give me your word on that."

I hesitated, then nodded. "Very well," I said. "But at least tell me your name."

"My name is Jamie," he said.

I held out my hand to him, and we shook hands as friends.

"Very well, Jamie," I said. "I give you my word I will keep your secret. But if you need my help, then let me know."

As I watched Jamie leave and head back up to the main deck, my heart felt heavy for him and his sadness. I determined that I should watch Simnel on his behalf, and when the time came make sure that Simnel would do him no further harm.

As Uncle Rufus had predicted, the Conference of the captains of the fleet was not a long one. By noon they were returning to their own vessels, and orders were being given out among our crew. We were going to sail right into Cadiz harbour and attack the Spanish fleet where they lay moored. Right into the heart of the Spanish King's fleet itself! My position was to be down on the gundeck, helping keep a supply of cannonballs to the gunners.

"Go and find Obadiah Jones," one of the mates instructed me. "You will be with his gun team."

I hastened below in search of Mr Jones. I had met the man when I joined the ship at Dover, as well as his second in charge, Mr Parsons.

Obadiah Jones was by one of the cannon, pouring gunpowder into the mouth of the gun. Gil Parsons stood beside him, holding a ramrod (a long pole covered with wool and leather at one end) at the ready.

"The mate says I am to report to you, Mr Jones, to be on your gun team," I said.

"Good," nodded Mr Jones in acknowledgement. "Your companions on our team are Mr Percy, Mr Adams and Mr Roberts."

The three other men in the gun team were among those who had come aboard at Plymouth and I had not known them by name. One was a dark-haired man, one fair, and the other completely bald. I bowed to the three men, who nodded back to me.

"Not that there will be time for talking once the action starts," said Mr Jones. "But if there is danger, at least you will know whose name to call."

Turning to the other men there he asked: "Have any of you seen action with a gun crew afore?"

"I have," nodded Mr Roberts.

"Then you know the dangers," said Mr Jones. To Mr Percy, Mr Adams and myself, he said: "When I fire, keep back from the cannon else the recoil will take your arm or leg off. But not too far back. I want cannonballs ready for me as fast as I load the powder, is that clear?"

We all nodded.

"Gil here," and Mr Jones gestured at Mr Parsons, "is our ramrod man. Keep out of his way so he has got free passage to the mouth of the gun."

Then Mr Jones loaded a cannonball into the gun's mouth and Mr Parsons finished the job by pushing the ball down inside the barrel of the cannon with his ramrod.

"Right," announced Mr Jones. "Now we are all ready for the Spaniards."

Suddenly I felt the ship list sharply, and then move as our anchor was raised. We were on our way. Try as

I might to make myself calm, I could not but feel my heart pounding in my chest with a mixture of fear and excitement.

Through the open gunports of the gunnery deck I saw that no flags were yet raised on any ships in our fleet. I supposed Captain Drake's plan was to make the Spanish in Cadiz think that no enemy warship would be so bold as to sail direct into the harbour, and that we must be Spanish or Portuguese ships.

As we sailed towards the port, all along the gundeck the cannons were being braced with ropes to hold them steady. We were coming in under full sail between the harbour walls. I felt the boat slow against the waves, and I knew that the sail had been furled. Mr Jones said that we had been turned into the outgoing tide to slow us down.

Now I saw the Spanish ships clearly. Even from this distance I could see the men on board scurrying around the upper decks, and knew they were hurrying to their stations, ready for battle. But we had been too quick for them.

"FIRE!" roared Mr Belson from the centre of the gundeck.

Jones thrust his smoking taper into the back of the cannon and sparks flared from out of the hole. "Back!"

Jones shouted, and we all leapt away – just in time because a loud explosion filled the area around us with smoke, bright sparks and flames. I could not see if we had hit any of the Spanish ships, all I could see was smoke. Then I saw Jones was already putting more gunpowder into the mouth of the cannon and was holding out his hand, ready to receive a cannonball. I reached down into the wooden box and grabbed at a ball, but it was as if it was nailed to the others and I could not lift it out.

"Stand aside," grunted Percy, the bald man, and he reached in and picked up the heavy metal ball as if it was made of wood. He passed it to Jones, who slid it into the mouth of the cannon, and Parsons rammed the ball further down into the cannon. Then Jones pushed a piece of wadding into the mouth of the cannon, and Parsons pushed that down hard as well.

Once again, Jones picked up a smouldering taper from the side of the cannon and thrust it into the touch-hole. "Back!" he shouted, and once more we all stepped back as the cannon fired, the great machine hurtling back towards us at speed, barely caught by the ropes that held it.

As the smoke cleared from the gunport I could see men diving off the Spanish ships into the sea, desperate to escape from the English cannonballs hurtling towards their ships. Their ships were taking a battering as ball after ball smashed into their sides, some ripping into their rigging and bringing their sails crashing down on to the decks to add to the chaos.

"Thomas, you just keep me supplied with powder," said Jones, pointing to the other side of the cannon where the powder was kept in a small keg.

"I am sorry, the cannonballs were too heavy for me, Mr Jones," I said.

He winked at me in a friendly fashion. "Do not worry yourself on it, Thomas," he said. "After a few more months at sea you will be juggling with them."

We then swung into a rhythm, with Percy, Adams and Roberts keeping the cannon supplied with the heavy cannonballs, which Parsons pushed home into the cannon. In between each shot I passed fresh gunpowder to Jones, who poured just the right measure into the cannon.

I noticed that none of our shots hit the ships below the waterline to sink them. Jones had said that Captain Drake was intent on keeping the Spanish ships afloat, and I soon discovered the reason why. When the order came from Mr Belson to "Cease fire!", the *Elizabeth Bonaventura* put on sail again. We suddenly began to move at speed towards the nearest and largest Spanish ship. I could see that the other ships in our fleet were doing the same.

"All hands on deck!" roared the voice of one of Mr Pugh's mates.

Obadiah Jones wiped the sweat from his eyes with his hand, the movement leaving a trail of black sludge across his face. "Plunder time, boys!" he grinned, the few white teeth that he had shining through the blackness of his face. I imagined that my face must be just as black from the gunpowder and smoke.

On deck the boarding parties were being prepared as we moved nearer and nearer the large Spanish vessel. The men were standing by the starboard rail holding ropes with hooks on the end ready in their hands. Among them was Uncle Rufus.

The soldiers we had taken aboard had assembled at the rail in two ranks, one behind the other, their bows aimed at the Spanish ship, some using longbows, some crossbows.

The deck of the enemy ship looked to be in disarray. The sails were spread around the deck, rigging had tumbled down, broken wooden spars lay everywhere. Smoke hung over the vessel like a dark cloud, and small fires burnt here and there. Some of the men on board were trying to put them out, but it was a useless task. As we drew closer, some of the Spaniards lined up against the rail of their ship, swords drawn, ready to defend their crippled vessel against our boarding party.

Mr Pugh was standing with the rest of the senior officers in the fo'c'sle and he called to our archers: "Fire arrows!"

From all along our starboard side the first rank of our archers let loose their shafts. A number of the Spaniards fell down, arrows sticking out from their bodies.

"Fire arrows!" shouted Mr Pugh again, and the second rank of our archers let fly.

This time the surviving Spaniards gave up the fight, rushed to the far side of their ship and began leaping into the water. One or two hesitated, wondering whether to remain and fight, but as we drew closer, they ran for their lives.

"Ropes!" called Mr Pugh.

Rufus and the other men by the starboard rail swung the hooked end of their ropes back, and then let them soar high into the air. The ropes flew across the distance between the two ships, and hooked on to the Spanish vessel.

"Furl sails!" called Mr Berry, and our sails were rapidly pulled up as the men began hauling on the ropes.

We were now side on side with the Spanish ship. I looked around and everywhere in the harbour I could see our sister warships carrying out the same manoeuvre, each capturing a Spanish ship of their own.

In the distance I spied our merchant ships lurking just outside the harbour, ready to take whatever treasures we should find.

Then came the crunching sound of wood against wood, and the familiar voice of Drake himself, cheerfully calling out, "Take it, lads!"

A great roar went up from the sailors around me and I found myself dragged along with them as they pushed forward, cheering loudly. I clambered over the rails of both ships, and down on to the Spanish deck.

Jones and Parsons, along with other members of our crew, had their swords and knives out in case a Spaniard should still be lurking on board, but it soon became obvious that there was no one left to defend the ship. I spied Simnel, knife at the ready, prowling the enemy deck, and decided it was safer to keep my distance from him. I looked around to see if Jamie had come aboard the Spanish vessel, but there was no sign of him.

Seeing Stevens head below decks, I decided to follow him down to the officers' cabins to look for gold and jewels. But there was such a crowd battling in the small rooms that it was impossible for me to get in. I gave up and climbed down to the cargo holds, where I helped the other men carry the boxes and barrels up to the main deck and back to the *Bonaventura*.

Drake had joined us on board the Spanish ship by this time, and was pacing around the main deck, inspecting the damage. With him he had Mr Harris, the carpenter, and Mr Berry, the Master. As I carried a box over to the *Bonaventura* I overheard Drake sizing up the vessel.

"Can it be repaired, Mr Harris?" asked Drake.

"It can, but 'tis just a merchant ship," Harris replied, nodding.

"I agree," put in Mr Berry. "'Tis warships we are in need of."

Drake smiled. "My views exactly, gentlemen," he said. "But 'tis good to hear you experts accord with me. Very well, Mr Berry, give the orders to bring the booty aboard the *Bonaventura*, and then fire this ship. That will be one less for the Spanish to raid England with."

And so the order was given, and the prizes and plunder we took from the enemy ship were carried over to the *Bonaventura*. Then fires were started on the Spanish ship below decks, our ropes were cast off, our sails unfurled, and we sailed away. Already flames could be seen flickering up from the hatchways as the ship we had plundered began to burn. As Captain Drake had said, it would be one less Spanish ship to threaten England.

As we headed for the mouth of the harbour and the open sea, I heard a voice call my name. It was Jamie. He came hurrying over to me and we hugged each other, pleased that we had both survived this, our very first battle.

"Where were you during the fighting?" I asked.

"I was aloft on the sails," said Jamie. "And you?"

"One of the gun crews," I said proudly. "I kept powder supplied for Mr Jones."

As we sailed out of the harbour Jamie and I stood and looked back. We could see that some of our fleet were towing Spanish warships behind them that they had taken as prizes. Others had done as we did and set the ship they had plundered afire. We left the blaze behind us, and I felt myself swell with pride. I had fought with Drake at Cadiz. We had defeated and burnt the Spanish fleet. We had saved England from invasion, and we had taken plunder. I, Thomas Hobbs, was now a fully fledged battle-hardened sailor of the English fleet.

*May – June 1587*

After the raid on Cadiz our fleet reassembled just off the coast of Spain, and Captain Drake and the other officers set to work dividing up the spoils. Everything was priced, from the cargoes of wheat and iron that had been taken, to the barrels of oil, biscuits and dried fruits. The weapons that had been taken were also counted. Then, when everything had been listed and their value added up, the plunder was spread around the different ships of the fleet.

Crews were reassigned from our own ships to take charge of the six captured Spanish warships, with carpenters being put aboard to carry out repairs as we sailed. They would be added to the English fleet to bolster its numbers.

I thought we had done well and would be heading back to England, but it seemed what we had achieved was not enough for Captain Drake.

"Iron and wheat and the like is all very well and will fetch a good price back in England," Rufus told me, "but what Captain Drake likes is stuff that is as good as money with a lot less bulk. Gold and jewels."

And so, on 22nd May, after taking on supplies of fresh water and wood for repairs, Captain Drake decided to split the fleet, sending half of the ships sailing back to England with the plunder and the news of our victory. Meanwhile, the *Elizabeth Bonaventura* would lead eight other ships westward towards the Azores in search of Spanish treasure.

According to Uncle Rufus, the Azores were a small group of islands far out in the Atlantic Ocean that the Spanish had taken as their own. They were a stopping-off point for Spanish ships going to and from the Americas.

"The Americas are lands where lumps of solid gold can be just picked up by a man walking," said Rufus. "Mind, the natives there are suspicious now and do not give up their gold so easy, but that is because the Spanish treated the natives so badly."

Our journey took us far out into the Atlantic, a thousand miles towards the Americas, the New World. Here the seas were rougher than off the coast of Spain, and far rougher than they had been back by the English coast.

The journey to the Azores took us two weeks of hard sailing, with everything on our decks that could move lashed down with ropes. Waves 30-feet high soared up alongside us, sometimes reaching as high as our mast before crashing down, sending water cascading across our deck, to pour back out into the sea through the wooden rails. Our ship, and the other eight of our small fleet, was tossed about like a feather in a gale.

During those two weeks I did my best to keep an eye on Jamie. I knew the kind of bully that Simnel was, and that his pleasure lay in beating Jamie and making him do his bidding, but I also knew that Simnel was wary of me because of my uncle. Although I had made a promise not to tell Rufus about Simnel's mistreatment of Jamie, I thought that if I stayed close, then, perhaps, Simnel would keep away from the boy. This seemed to work for a while, but there were a few times when I came upon Jamie hiding behind a box or a coil of rope, and saw the bruises on his face and knew that Simnel had been at him again. When Jamie was asked about these bruises he lied and said he had fallen and knocked himself. Such was the hard pace of life on board, with all of us working to keep the ship on a straight course, that the rest of the crew had no time to look deeper into Jamie's answers.

On the morning of the 8th June I heard the lookout from the top of the main mast call: "Land ahoy! Land ahoy!"

"The Azores!" said Rufus joyfully. "Spanish gold will be here in plenty, you can count on it, my boy!"

As we came nearer the land I saw a magnificently painted large ship floating at anchor, moored about a mile off the coast of the largest island. As word spread about our vessel, the crew crowded on the port side of the deck as we came in, eager to get a view of it and make out what it was.

"'Tis the *San Felipe*!" said Stevens in my ear, and there was no mistaking the delight in his voice.

"Is it a special ship?" I asked.

"No more a special ship than we could wish to encounter," chuckled Rufus. "We are lucky indeed! The *San Felipe* is nothing else but the King of Spain's very own ship."

"Let us hope she is returning from the Americas and not on her outwards journey," said Stevens. "If she is on her way home, she will be laden with treasure!"

The orders were given to bring the *Elizabeth*

*Bonaventura* alongside the *San Felipe*. At the same time four of the other warships from our fleet moved out so that she was surrounded on all sides. The whole time we were carrying out this manoeuvre I expected the crew on board the Spanish ship to fire at us, but no shots came. And I could see that the Spanish ship only had a skeleton crew on board. The rest of her crew must have been ashore.

"Why do they not defend themselves?" I asked Rufus as we drew nearer.

"They have seen Drake's flag and, to the Spanish, Captain Drake is the very devil. 'Tis bad enough for them he is a Protestant who hates Catholics with a venom, but even worse for them, they know that Captain Drake never loses a battle. They say that he must have sold his soul to the Devil. They are surrounded, they know they have already lost their ship. Why lose their lives as well? If they surrender they know 'tis likely that Captain Drake will release them ashore unharmed."

It went exactly as Rufus said it would. A white flag was run up the mast of the Spanish king's ship in sign of surrender. We drew alongside and tied up, then raiding parties went aboard, while the few Spanish sailors stood with their hands in the air and watched.

I went aboard with a party that included Rufus and Stevens, led by Mr Pugh. Mr Pugh could speak a few words of Spanish and he questioned the sailors as to where they had been and what they were carrying. On the promise of safe passage to the shore if they helped us, and death if they did not, the Spanish showed us where everything was. It was a magnificent haul: case after case of gold and jewels. It was just as Stevens had hoped, the *San Felipe* was on its way back to Spain from the Southern Americas.

As we brought the chests aboard the *Elizabeth Bonaventura*, we were watched by a smiling Captain Drake, and Mr Nichols. I was surprised to see that for once even Mr Nichols's face had the ghost of a smile on it. I heard him say to Captain Drake: "A goodly haul, Francis. Today a great blow has been struck against the Pope and his forces."

"And a great sum has been lodged in our purses, Philip!" laughed Drake.

The Spanish sailors were set down in longboats and allowed to row for the shore and safety. Then a skeleton crew drawn from our own nine ships was put aboard the *San Felipe* as her crew. Once that was done, the anchors of the fleet were raised and we turned for the north. We were going home.

✝ ✝ ✝

We arrived back in Plymouth on 26th June. Once we were tied up there was great jostling on board to collect our pay and be off the ship, on land once more. After nearly four months at sea, I was looking forward to getting home and seeing Mam and Mary and young Daniel. (I was even looking forward to seeing Dad again, especially as I would be putting money into his hands.) Still, I made a point of searching out Jamie before I made my way back to London.

"Well, we have made it back to England," I said. "What will you do now? Look for another ship?"

Jamie shook his head. "No," he said. "I shall be going straight home to Bristol. This once on board ship has been enough for me. In future I will only be in places where, if things go wrong for me, I can run away. At sea there is nowhere to run."

"I am sorry you suffered as you did," I said. "Despite my promise to you, I should have told my uncle about Simnel."

Again Jamie shook his head. "No. It was better the way it was. At least I knew there was one person on board the *Bonaventura* I could count on as a friend, and for that I thank you from the bottom of my heart, Thomas."

As we shook hands and said goodbye, I saw the figure of Simnel appear from the hatchway, his bundle of belongings over his shoulder. The villain looked at us and glared, and if looks could kill I would have been struck dead there and then. I saw Jamie tremble, but I firmly gripped his hand and said, "Have no more fear of him, Jamie. The voyage is over. You will go your own way and there is no need for you to see him ever again."

Jamie gave a smile and nodded. "You are right, Thomas. I wish you well in the future and hope that one day we will meet again."

Jamie and I collected our belongings, and then joined the queue of men lined up on deck to pass the purser's table. One by one our names were called out – each man stepped forward and had his wages counted out for him and put in a leather bag. Then he was free to leave. As cabin boys, we were near the end of the list, but Uncle Rufus and Stevens waited for me. Jamie's name was called first, and after he collected his money, he waved me goodbye and hurried off the ship, taking care to slip past Simnel. Then it was my turn.

"Thomas Hobbs!" called out the purser's mate, and I hurried to the table.

"Thomas Hobbs, cabin boy," said the purser. "Wages of five shillings a month for four months is 20 shillings, plus 30 shillings as his share of the prize. A total of 50 shillings."

Fifty shillings! I was rich! This was more money than I had ever seen in my life! With this money we could move out of Garlands. This money would pay the rent on a proper house of our own for over a year. And there would probably be enough over to buy presents for Mam and Mary and Daniel, and something for Dad.

"Sign or make your mark against your name," said the purser. I made my mark, took my leather pouch and joined Rufus and Stevens.

"I am rich!" I told them. "Fifty shillings!"

They looked at one another and laughed at my pleasure.

"See, I told you you would get rich with Captain Drake," chuckled Rufus. Then his face became serious and he said warningly: "But getting it is one thing, Thomas. Hanging on to it is another business altogether."

"Listen to what your uncle says," added Stevens, also looking serious. " 'Tis a hard business keeping hold of money."

"Beware if you go into a tavern," warned Rufus. "Avoid strong drink. And avoid people who see you have got money and claim to be your friends. Many's the sailor who has come back from the sea, his pockets filled with gold, and the next morning he has woken up with his pockets empty and his brain addled because he fell into bad company. Beware, Thomas, there are thieves and pickpockets everywhere. Is that not right, Stevens?"

"Aye, Rufus, 'tis true right enough," nodded Stevens. "It has happened to me a few times, I regret to say, after a long hard voyage."

"Well, it will not happen to me," I told them. "I am not waiting to spend even one night here in Plymouth. I am off this afternoon to find a cart to take me home to London, and to Mam and Dad."

"A cart?" chuckled Stevens. "Why, boy, you can afford a seat on a coach!"

"Ah, but if I did that I would be advertising to all the ruffians on the way that I had money," I said. "If I travel by cart they will think I am just a poor boy heading for the town by the only way a poor person can. That way no one will think I have got money about my person."

Stevens laughed admiringly. "You have brains,

Thomas, I will say that for you," he said. "Ain't that so, Rufus?"

In the distance I heard a bell chime the hour of ten o'clock. If I could find a carter who would take me, I could set off before noon, and in three days, four at most, I would be in London again, back with my family. At that moment, I wished I had learned to write so that I could send them a letter telling them I was well, having come back safe and with riches in my pocket.

I bade a fond goodbye to Uncle Rufus and Stevens. They said they would be staying in Plymouth to look for work to tide them over until their next voyage. I said I hoped they would call to London and see me there. I told them I hoped to be able to move my family into better premises as soon as I returned to London, but I would leave a message at Garlands saying where we had moved to. With that, I set off for the main market to look for a cart that might be heading for London.

As I walked through the market, I was sure that someone was behind me, keeping pace with my steps. But each time I turned round there was no one. For one moment I wondered if Simnel had come to wreak his revenge, but I shrugged the thought off. I was on dry land now. Jamie was safe and on his way back home, and so was I.

I asked about and found a carter who was transporting bales of silk and cloth to London that very afternoon, right to Moorgate itself. I arranged I would meet him again just after one o'clock, and then I set off to get provisions for the journey just some bread and cheese and ale would keep my belly full. I would save having a proper meal until I got back to my family. Then I would spend money on such a spread of celebration as would make my mam's eyes fill with tears of happiness.

I cut through a narrow cobbled alley, heading for a tavern to purchase a bottle of ale, when I saw a sudden movement out of the corner of my eye. I began to turn, when something smashed down on the back of my head. Everything was pain and darkness.

I do not know how long I must have been lying there but I remember sounds around me, voices getting louder, someone saying, "Is he dead?"

I opened my eyes and saw a woman bending over me, a look of concern on her face.

"His eyes are open," said a man's voice. "Come, let us be moving."

"But there is blood on his head," said the woman.

She reached out her hand towards me, but the man stopped her sharply.

"Leave him," he said. "He is just a guttersnipe. He is alive. His family will look after him."

Then he pulled her roughly away from me and I heard their footsteps hurrying along the alley. I struggled up to a sitting position. My head hurt. I put my hand to it, and saw blood on my fingers.

My money! The thought cut through the fog of pain in my brain and I reached into my breeches for my cloth where I had tied my bag of coins. It was gone! I sat there on the cobbles, overwhelmed by misery. I could not believe this had happened to me.

Somehow I forced myself to my feet. My head ached, I felt dizzy and I nearly fell again, but I knew I had to find Uncle Rufus and tell him what had happened. He would be able to help find the villain – or villains – who had done this, I felt sure.

Uncle Rufus and Stevens were still by the docks, sitting on barrels, watching the ships arriving.

"Thomas!" called Rufus merrily when he saw me. His expression changed when he saw the look on my face, and the blood that had trickled down from my forehead.

He stood up and sat me down on his barrel, and

then he and Stevens listened in horror as I told them what had happened.

"Did you not see who did it?" asked Stevens.

"Not one whit!" I said, feeling tears begin to well up in my eyes. "Why rob *me* of all people? I do not look like a rich sailor and I kept my money hidden. I told the carter who was taking me to London that I had scarce but a penny to pay him."

Rufus and Stevens exchanged grim looks.

"Maybe 'twas someone from the ship," muttered Stevens.

"Nay!" Rufus shook his head. "Who would rob a shipmate?"

"Simnel," I said. "I am sure of it! I am certain he was following me while I was in the market this morning. He hated me and swore he would have his own back for the way I defended the other cabin boy against him."

And then I told Rufus and Stevens of how Jamie had suffered at Simnel's hands during the voyage, and how I had kept a lookout for the boy, but he had made me promise to say nothing for fear of his life. Rufus's face grew dark with anger.

"The scum!" snarled Rufus. "I tell you, Thomas, if 'twas Simnel who did this to you, then he shall answer for this with his life," and he got up, ready to go in search of him.

"Wait!" Stevens said, and grabbed Rufus's arm. "'Tis not enough to have suspicion before we accuse him. We need proof."

"We have proof!" raged Rufus. "Thomas saw him watching him!"

Stevens shook his head. "Watching is not the same as attacking," he pointed out. Turning to me, he asked: "How long before you were attacked did you see Simnel?"

I tried to think, but my brains still felt scrambled.

"Perhaps an hour before," I said.

"An hour," said Stevens shaking his head. "It is not much in the way of proof, Rufus."

"We will have proof as soon as I get my hands on the villain!" snapped my uncle. "A confession! Come!"

And with that Rufus stormed off, heading for the nearest tavern, with Stevens and myself in tow.

We spent the next hour trawling through the alehouses of Plymouth, looking for Simnel, and asking our shipmates if they had sight of him. Finally we tracked him down, drinking with some of our old crew in "The Hammer".

It was a small dark noisy room, packed with men,

and the air was heavy with the smell of ale.

"Why, what have we here?!" called out Simnel cheerily as he saw us approaching, pushing our way through the crush. "All shipmates together!"

"Do not smile at me, Simnel!" snapped Rufus angrily. "I am here to demand you give this boy his money back."

"Money?" laughed Simnel. "And why should I have the whelp's money?"

"Because you took it from him, after beating him over the head from behind like the coward you are!"

"That is a bold charge to make, Rufus Clark," growled another sailor called Hawkins. "How do you know it was Simnel who did it?"

"Because beating a child is the sort of snakelike thing that he would do. Like he beat Jamie, the other cabin boy. Boys are all he can take, he is too much of a coward to stand up to a man!"

Simnel scowled at this and leapt to his feet, kicking his chair over as he did so.

"Coward, am I?" he roared. "Well I will take you on, Rufus Clark, aye and the whole three of you!"

"Wait!" shouted Hawkins. "Afore we have murder here, when did this attack take place?"

Everyone looked at me. I struggled to work out the

time when I was attacked, and then declared, "It must have been between noon and one o'clock this afternoon, for I remember the clock striking twelve when I talked to the carter."

Hawkins turned to Rufus. "If that is so then there is no robber here, Rufus Clark," he said. "For I have been here with Simnel since he joined us at eleven this morning, and I can swear to that, and so can these men with us. He did not rob the boy."

As all the other crew nodded in agreement, my heart sank. Simnel turned to me with a leer. "Well, my little whelp, looks like I am in need of an apology from you," he smirked. "And you, too, Rufus Clark."

I could not speak. My eyes were filling with tears and, desperate not to let the men see me cry, I turned and pushed my way as quickly as I could out of the tavern. Behind me I heard Simnel call loudly, "I want an apology, cabin boy!"

Then I was outside in the street.

I felt a hand on my shoulder. It was Stevens.

"It *was* Simnel who did it!" I insisted, and now the tears came, pouring down my face in anger and frustration.

"Aye, I believe it was," muttered Stevens. "I wager he has put the finger on you to some robbers and will share the spoils with them. He will have made sure he had a story to account for the time when you were attacked. But we have no proof of this, just a feeling. And without proof, we have nothing."

"I have nothing," I said, and I wiped my tears away. All those weeks at sea, all that work, all that hardship, all the promises I had made and the presents I was going to buy for Mam and Mary and Daniel, and now I had nothing. Not a penny.

Rufus joined us, his face flushed with anger. "That scum!" he said. "He laughed at me! Says he will put a justice on me for false charges! I ought to tear his head off!"

"Stay, Rufus," cautioned Stevens. "You do not want to end up in jail. 'Twould be even worse injustice."

Uncle Rufus and Stevens did what they could to cheer me up but by now I had missed my appointment with the carter bound for London. Not that I fancied going back and facing my family after what had just happened to me. I had never felt so wretched and sorry for myself in my life.

Rufus and Stevens helped me find another carter transporting cargo to London, this one a cartload of dried fish, which stank to high heaven. They also gave me some money, five shillings, which was still more than I had ever had in my life, but far short of the 50 shillings I had earned at sea. The two men stayed with me until I finally set off for London, to make sure that no further trouble befell me.

*July – December 1587*

The journey home took six days, and by the end of it my nose and clothes were so filled with the smell of dried fish that I never wanted to eat or see another fish again.

It was strange returning home after my four months at sea. Cramped though conditions had been on the *Elizabeth Bonaventura*, Garlands seemed even smaller as I stepped through the door and climbed the stairs to our rooms. The whole family was there, and when I appeared at the door, Mary gave a squeal of delight. "Thomas!" she yelled. "Mam! Dad! Thomas has returned home!"

Mam and Dad came out from the small room and Mam rushed towards me, her arms open wide.

"My Thomas!" she cried happily, and crushed me to her. "I thought you had been drowned at sea! Oh, it is so good to see you again! We heard all about the raid on the Spanish king's ships in Cadiz!"

"Yes, did you really attack the Spanish fleet and set it on fire, Thomas?" asked Mary.

"Yes, we really did," I nodded. "And then we sailed on to the Azores and we took the Spanish king's ship as a prize!"

"So, you *have* become a pirate, like your uncle," snapped Dad.

"Not a pirate," I protested. "We did it in the service of the Queen!"

"And now you have come home with riches in your pockets, I suppose," Dad said sourly.

I hung my head. "I have only five shillings," I said.

Mam looked at me, surprised. "Five shillings, Thomas, for all those months away?"

I told them what had happened to me in Plymouth, how I had been attacked and robbed of my 50 shillings wages.

Mary gaped. "Fifty shillings!" she echoed. "A fortune!"

"A fortune he does not have, like most sailors I know," growled Dad. "But then, if you work and live among thieves and pirates, what do you expect? So now you have come back to live off my humble wages, have you?"

The scornful tone in his voice made me angry. I had endured hardship after hardship, put my life at risk to save England from the Spanish, and had been robbed and nearly murdered at the end of it, and there was no thanks for me in his welcome, just hard-heartedness as always.

"No," I told him proudly. "I will live here and pay my way only until such time as I can get on board a ship again." I gave Mam the five shillings that Rufus and Stevens had given me. "Here, Mam, these are for my keep. Tomorrow I will go to Moorgate and find work to tide me over, until a ship becomes free."

As true as my word, early next morning I made my way to the cloth market. On my way there I heard a joyful shout of "Thomas!" and I turned and saw my friend William Baker, running towards me.

"'Tis good to see you again, Thomas!" said William, shaking my hand vigorously. "We heard the reports of Drake's fleet and the attack on the Spanish in Cadiz. What was it like? Were men killed? Did you take prisoners? Did you take much treasure?"

William was so keen to hear the details that his words began to run into one another, and I had to hold up my hand to stop him.

"Calm down, William," I said. "I will tell you all in

good time, but first I must get to Moorgate and see if Mr Petty has any work for me."

William looked at me, astonished. "Work?" he echoed. "But we heard that Drake's ship took much Spanish plunder. Did you not get a share?"

"I did, but I was robbed of it," I sighed. And then I swore William to secrecy and told him how I had been robbed by bandits who I was sure were in league with a villain called Simnel.

When I finished my story, William's face looked as angry as mine must have done on the day of the robbery. "This Simnel is a villain!" he spat. "He should be hung!"

"Indeed he should," I agreed, "but there is no proof. He is a clever villain. One that I hope I never lay eyes on again. Now, let us to the market and get our work before others take it, and after work I will come home with you and tell you all about my adventures."

Because I had been one of Sir Francis Drake's crew, Mr Petty was pleased to find work for me, sorting cloth. He was delighted to be able to tell his customers about me: one of Sir Francis Drake's crew who had actually been with the great man in the attack on the Spanish fleet, and in the taking of the Spanish king's ship. Because of the attention it got his stall, Mr Petty was quite happy for me to work less and talk more, keeping his customers spellbound with my stories of life on board Drake's ship.

William was also happy to hang around Mr Petty's stall listening to my tales, prompting me from time to time as I spoke. "Tell them what Captain Drake said to you when he first met you!" he would say. Eventually, the people he worked for got fed up with him hanging around Mr Petty's stall, and he was forced to stay away.

I was quite delighted to be paid to be an entertainment – it was a lot easier than the heavy work of hauling bales of cloth and rags. However, after one week, Mr Petty's customers had heard all my tales, as had the friends they bought along to hear me, and so it was soon back to the heavy work.

Over the next few months, I worked on the stall for two pennies a day. But when October came and the daylight became shorter, I began to work fewer hours and so my wages went down to a penny and a halfpenny a day. By November I was down to earning just a penny. The bad feeling between Dad and me worsened, and he began muttering about people who ate more in food than the money they brought into the house. I forced myself to keep my mouth shut and not respond to his remarks.

William was still keen to hear me tell my tales of my life at sea, but the further my time at sea receded into the past the more it seemed to me as if it had just been a dream on my part.

There were more beheadings of traitors who had been involved in the latest plot to kill the Queen, but no one I had heard of before. A Lord this and a Sir that. Still, William and I went along to London Bridge to look at the heads as soon as they went up on spikes. William was as excited as ever to see the blood and bones visible on the necks of the victims, but for me, having been in battle and seen men killed and injured, the spectacle did not now hold the same fascination.

The arrival of Uncle Rufus broke through the winter gloom. He arrived one evening in early November, just as we were about to have supper, which caused my dad to make a remark about people who arrive just as food touches the table. Rufus was used to my dad's comments about him and, as usual, decided to ignore them and just be jolly with the rest of the family.

"I thought I would call and see how young Thomas was doing after his terrible tragedy in Plymouth," he said in between mouthfuls of bread dipped in gravy. He smiled approvingly at Mam. "This is delicious, Susan! Much better than we ever get on board ship! Ain't that true, Thomas?"

Mam smiled, pleased at Rufus's praise. Dad just scowled.

"Proper meat and good bread is what honest people ashore eat," he said. "We may not have gold and jewels stolen from foreign merchant ships, but what we have in our mouths is honestly earned."

Rufus pretended not to hear Dad's barbed words, but used them to mention the reason for his visit. "Talking of the sea, John, it is one of the reasons I have come," he said. "As well as to see how my sister and niece and nephews are keeping, of course."

Dad scowled again and said nothing, just ate.

"I hear there is trouble coming from Spain again," Rufus continued.

"There cannot be much trouble," I said. "We destroyed the Spanish fleet, after all."

"What can be destroyed can be made again," said

Rufus. "The word is that the King of Spain has been given money by the Pope to build another Armada."

"No!" said Mam, horrified.

"Yes, Susan," nodded Rufus. "And an even bigger Armada than before. Stronger. Bigger ships. 'Tis said the Spanish have been building it ever since we came back. With their new ships, 'twill be one of the biggest armed fleets ever assembled, so they say."

"And is it to be attacked?" I asked, hope springing up in my breast. "Does Captain Drake want crew? For I am ready," I said, adding fiercely, "and this time no robber will take my wages from me."

"No!" snapped my dad. "This time you will die before you get any wages!"

"Hush, John," Mam appealed to him. "Please do not talk of death that way! We do not want to invite it."

"I hear Captain Drake is to be part of a fleet now being assembled," Rufus continued. "Whether we are to attack the Spaniards, or to defend our coast, I do not know. All I do know is that it will happen, Thomas, and when it does, I will send for you, if you so wish."

"Yes, I wish indeed, Uncle Rufus!" I said fervently. I turned to Dad and appealed to him: "Dad, I know you do not approve of the sea, but I feel it is where I belong, where I feel at home."

Dad opened his mouth as if to say something sharp, but instead, he said simply, "If you feel your home is the sea, Thomas, then so be it. The sooner you go there, the better." With that he turned and went into the small room, shutting the door behind him, as he always did when he was in an unhappy mood.

Rufus gave Mam and me a sad smile. "I am sorry, Susan," he said. "I always seem to bring strife to this house when I come."

Mam shook her head. "No, Rufus," she said. "'Tis just the way John is. He is a good man at heart but set in his ways. And his ways are not yours, and never will be. He will come round to Thomas going to sea one day, I am sure."

Over the next two months the rumours and stories about the new Spanish Armada began to build up. Once again I became a centre of attraction at Mr Petty's stall because I had sailed with Drake and taken part in the destruction of the first fleet. Now, with the prospect of an even larger Armada sailing for England, I was more popular than ever. The Armada was said to be bringing Spanish troops to kill all the Protestants in

England and people wanted to talk to me and ask me what Drake was like as a man and as a fighter, and if I thought he could defeat the Spanish again.

"Drake and his fleet can defeat the Spanish again and again and again," I told them confidently. "We did it before, and we will do it every time it is necessary." But I could see from their faces that, however many times I said this, most of them were not convinced.

That Christmas, as fever about the Spanish invasion grew, people started to hoard things: dried food, clothes, wheat. Even Dad began to bring home meat from the butchery for Mam to smoke and dry so that it could be stored. It was as if everyone expected the world to end at any moment, and they wanted to be well prepared with supplies if it did. There was no doubt in anyone's mind: a major war with Spain was just weeks away. And I could not wait to get out on to the open sea on Drake's ship and fight in it.

As good as his word, soon after the start of the new year, Uncle Rufus arrived at Garlands.

"We are sent for, Thomas!" he announced triumphantly. "Captain Drake bids us make speed for Plymouth where his fleet is assembling!"

"Why Plymouth?" I asked. "Why not Dover, as before?"

"Oh, there is a fleet assembling at Dover, right enough," said Rufus. "But Captain Drake wants to be nearest the action when the Spanish Armada arrives, and they will be coming from the south-west, that you can count on!"

This time I knew what lay ahead of me: the back-breaking work, the rolling waves, the smell of wood and sweat, the feel of sea-spray and the huge vistas of the night sky at sea. I felt desperate to be back out there and to have that sense of freedom and adventure.

Once more I took leave of my mam and Mary – Mam more tearful than she had been when I had gone before, and Mary more excited. My dad had gone to work by the time we were ready to leave, so I just told my mam to say goodbye to him for me. I did not expect he would miss me. Then Rufus and I set off for Plymouth.

Our journey took four days, not quite as long as it had on my last dreadful journey home. This time we were on a cart carrying dried beef, and the carter was an old friend of Rufus's.

"Dried beef for the fleet," Rufus said, gesturing to the back of the cart.

"Will we be on the *Elizabeth Bonaventura* again?" I asked.

Rufus shook his head. "Not this time," he said. "The *Bonaventura* is still being fitted out. Our ship for this adventure will be the *Revenge*. 'Tis smaller than the *Bonaventura*, but still a good size for all that."

When we arrived at Plymouth and went aboard ship, I discovered that once again we had only a skeleton crew. But I was glad to see that Stevens was amongst the men already on board.

"Well met, Thomas!" he greeted me. "I trust you have not lost your sea legs these long months ashore."

We shook hands and Stevens told me that Captain Drake had assembled the same group of senior officers as before to be about him: Mr Berry as Master, Mr

Pugh as bosun, Mr Belson as his master gunner, and Mr Harris as his carpenter.

Nervously I scanned the ship for a sign of Simnel's presence, but was relieved to find he was nowhere to be seen. I know Mam had always taught us to forgive our enemies, but what I believed Simnel had done to me – robbed me of every penny of my hard-earned money and left me for dead in the street – was something I could never forgive. Although I had no proof, I *knew* Simnel was guilty of the crime. I felt it in my bones. He may not have carried out the deed in person, but in my heart I knew him to be as guilty as if he had struck me down himself, and I never wanted to lay eyes on him again.

That evening, I discovered that our ship was not to be the flagship of the fleet for the forthcoming battle against the Spanish.

" 'Tis to be a bigger fight than any of us were ever in," Rufus explained to me. "Nigh on every ship from every port around England has been brought in. So, in this case, the flagship of the fleet is to be the *Ark*, which be the ship of Lord Charles Howard, the Earl of Effingham. As Lord High Admiral he has been put in overall charge of the fleet by none other than the Queen herself."

For the next five months we prepared the *Revenge,* getting stores on board, cleaning the guns, making sure the powder was kept dry. At 500 tons the ship was indeed slightly smaller than the *Bonaventura,* but she sat lower and snugger in the water and felt safer to be aboard.

All along the south coast lookouts were standing beside beacons, ready to set them alight at the first sight of the Spanish warships and send the warning along the coast. But by May there was still no sign of the Armada.

"Maybe the King of Spain has changed his mind," I said to Rufus one day.

"I hope not," replied Rufus. "This whole business between England and Spain needs to be decided one way or another and there is only one way to do it. One all-out battle, with one winner."

During all these months, Captain Drake rarely visited the ship. When he did, it was to check that we were all shipshape and ready to sail at a moment's notice, once the main crew came aboard. Whenever he appeared I thought he looked angry, and one day, as I was coiling a rope on deck, I learned the reason for his bad humour. He was in conversation with his chaplain, Mr Nichols.

"This waiting is driving me mad, Philip!" he grated. "We should be out there, on the high seas, attacking the Spanish before they can leave port, just the way we did at Cadiz. Bottle them up and burn them! Yet all the messages I send to the Queen urging her to let me loose seem to fall on deaf ears."

"The Queen has her own counsel," said Nichols.

"Yes!" snapped back Drake. "I bet 'tis those tight-purses at the Exchequer who tell her how much it cost to keep a ship at sea and so keep us bottled up here. I tell you, Philip, 'twill cost a sight more money to kick them out again if the Spaniards set foot on land!"

"They will not," said Nichols. "Of that I am assured. We have the finest sailors in the world spread all the way along our coastline defending it."

When I told Uncle Rufus and Stevens about this conversation, Rufus laughed. "If other tales I have heard be so, then 'tis true what the Captain says," he said. "The Queen may be the most wonderful queen on the world, but she do like to keep her purse-strings tight."

"I say let us wait and let the Spaniards come to us,"

put in Stevens. "Let them be worn and weary by the time they get to our shores. May the sea make them sick as dogs. Then we shall just pick them off at our leisure."

One day, right at the beginning of June, a messenger arrived on the quayside. I was swabbing the main deck and I saw him arrive at a gallop, tie up his horse, and run up the gangplank.

"Boy!" he called to me. "Where do I find Mr Berry, the Master of this ship? I have urgent news for him!"

"I will take you to him, sir," I said.

I left my mop and bucket and led the messenger down the hatchway, and then along the first deck to the stern of the ship. I showed the messenger in to Mr Berry's cabin, and then I hung around outside, keeping my ears peeled for the conversation.

"Mr Berry, I have a message for you from Sir Francis Drake," came the messenger's voice. "He commands you gather a full crew and prepare the ship. The Armada has left Spain and heads for England under full sail. With the wind as it is, they will be here by the end of the month. He will be joining you within the week, after he has met with the Queen. Here is his letter of orders, with his signature, for your sight."

"Thank you," said Mr Berry curtly.

Before the messenger could reappear from the cabin, I was already on my way to pass on the news to Rufus and Stevens. The Spanish Armada was on its way at last! The months of waiting were now at an end.

Over the next week our work increased tenfold. With the enemy on its way we were to make sure every gun was ready to fire, every rope was firm and safe, every barrel of gunpowder was dry. The stores of food and water were checked and double-checked. Meanwhile Mr Rook set out into the streets of Plymouth with the pressgangs to assemble the main crew. The *Revenge* needed a crew of 250, and at that moment we were just 50. With every other ship in the fleet needing men as well, the message was sent out to get men by any means. Day by day more men came aboard, many of them the rough sort that looked like they should have been in jail. Among the new arrivals I was glad to see Obadiah Jones and Gil Parsons returned to join the gun crew.

"Well met, young Thomas!" Obadiah hailed me as he and Gil walked up the gangplank.

"Good day to you, Mr Jones!" I replied, adding "And to you, Mr Parsons. I trust you are both well?"

Parsons grinned. "Well and poor, like all sailors, young Thomas," he chuckled. "Else why would we be here to risk our lives for measly pay?"

Obadiah Jones slapped his companion affectionately on the shoulder. "Enough of that talk, Gil," he said, turning to me. "Do not listen to what Gil says in jest. He would part with his own money to have a crack at the Armada. This is our chance to put an end to the King of Spain and his attacks on our great nation."

By the middle of June we had almost our full crew assembled. I kept a lookout in case Jamie had changed his mind and decided to sign up with Captain Drake again, but there was no sign of him. I assumed he had decided that once at sea really was enough, and he preferred life on land in Bristol.

And then one day the man I hated and most dreaded seeing again in the whole world set foot on board the *Revenge*. Simnel.

"Well, cabin boy!" he sneered as he saw me. "So, it seems we serve together again! I hope you earn well this time, for perhaps you will lend me money after this voyage is over!" And with that he laughed and went below to lay claim to his bed on the gundeck.

I watched Simnel go with hate in my heart. I had never felt as angry as I did at that moment. Now he had come back to taunt me with what he had done – and got away with. At that moment I vowed that I would finish this thing between Simnel and myself one way or another. I knew I would be no match for him in a straight fight, he being much stronger than I was, but I vowed to myself I would have my revenge on him.

## July 1588

Whether he had seen the look of hatred in my eyes and realized that I might be a danger to him, or whether he was just biding his time, Simnel stayed well away from me for the next few days. I decided to push him to the back of my thoughts and concentrate on my work of helping get the *Revenge* shipshape and ready for battle. But the battle that we were all expecting did not come. By 25th July there was still no sign of the Spanish ships.

"Will those Spanish never get here!" raged Uncle Rufus angrily one evening, when yet another day had passed without word of any sighting.

"I think maybe they are afeared of us, Rufus," commented Stevens. "Either that, or they have got lost on their way. Maybe they are halfway towards the Americas instead."

That night as I was going below decks, a hand grabbed me and pinned me against a wooden rail. The hideous snarling face of Simnel was pressed close to mine.

"You think because I have kept away from you this voyage that maybe you have seen the last of me," he snarled.

I could smell the rum on his breath and I wanted to be sick from the stale stink of it.

"You are drunk, Simnel!" I said. "Now leave me be or you will be the worse for it."

"Oh yes?" he sneered. "You will tell your uncle of me, will you? Well try it and see what good it may do you. With the Spanish on their way, Captain Drake needs every man he can get. He is not going to lose a good man like me because of the tales of a whelp like you!"

"Let go of me!" I said angrily, and I kicked at him, but in his drunken state he hardly felt my bare feet against his shins.

"Last time you accused me of robbery," Simnel snarled. "You blackened my name in front of my friends, and you never gave me that apology. Well I will have my revenge on you for that, young Thomas Hobbs, see if I do not. I will come for you when you are not expecting it. You will never shame me in public again, I promise you."

And then he released me and flung me down the stairs. I managed to catch the rail to stop myself from falling but when I looked up, Simnel was staggering away along the upper deck.

When I got down to my sleeping place Uncle Rufus was awake. He could tell there was something wrong.

"What is it, lad?" he asked, sitting up abruptly. "Has Simnel been at you again?"

I shook my head. "No," I lied. "I just stubbed my toe as I came down the stairs. I am angry at my own clumsiness."

Rufus chuckled. "If a stubbed toe is the worst you come out with from this affair, then you will be the luckiest boy in England," he said.

As I lay down to sleep, I realized I no longer needed Uncle Rufus's protection against Simnel. The man was a villain, but also a coward who only found courage when faced with children, or with drink inside him. But I was no longer just a boy. I knew in my heart that when the time came, I would be able to face Simnel on my own, and beat him.

On 27th July, Captain Drake came aboard in a great hurry with word that the Armada had been sighted off the Scilly Isles. Straight away the order was given to prepare the *Revenge* for sail, but a storm was blowing up with the wind driving so hard we could not even raise our sails for fear of them tearing. Instead we remained in Plymouth harbour.

Frustrating though it was, Stevens made me realize we had been lucky. "We think we are hard done by being stuck here in harbour," he said. "But think of those Spanish being tossed around in these winds out at sea off the Scillies. It will be taking some of the fight out of them, lad, that is for sure."

By the next day the storm had begun to die down, and on 29th July we were finally able to leave harbour and head out to sea, along with the *Hope*, *Victory*, *Triumph*, *Nonpareil* and some 45 other smaller ships. It had been said the Armada was made up of over a hundred ships, and here we were, at just half that number.

But somehow I felt confident of what we were about to do. I had sailed with Captain Drake before, I knew how fearless he was, and how that fearlessness struck awe into the hearts of his enemy. I had also seen for myself that there was none so capable of handling a large warship as Captain Drake, knowing how to use the winds and the tides to best advantage. If anyone could stop the Spanish fleet, it was he. And however small it might have been when compared to the Armada, this fleet was much bigger than our last. Still, our Master, Mr Berry, would need to keep his wits about him and a sharp eye on the signal flags being flown from the Admiral's flagship, the *Ark*, with the instructions to the fleet.

We sailed just out into the Channel, and then headed west, keeping the coast in view the whole time. Up in the crow's nest at the top of our mast our lookout was scanning the horizon. Two more days had passed since that first sighting of the Spaniards off the Scillies, and still yet no sign of them. A mist had started to roll in, and I wondered whether they had managed to slip past us and were even now on their way heading in to land further along the coast.

From the ship I could see the fires of the alarm beacons burning, sending up columns of smoke high into the sky. The first had been lit at the Lizard in Cornwall when word had first come that the Armada had been sighted at sea. That beacon had been the signal for the whole chain to be lit one by one as the flames from the previous one were spotted. Right across the country these huge fires were being lit, warning the population that the Spanish Armada was just off the coast. But it was nowhere to be seen.

✝ ✝ ✝

On the morning of Sunday 31st July, I was helping two sailors named Kelly and Matthews coil a length of rope, when we heard a shout from the lookout high up in the crow's nest. "Sails hoy!" We turned and looked and saw something on the horizon, emerging from the mist. In full sail, and with flags flying, it had to be the Spanish Armada.

"Glory be!" gasped Kelly. "There must been at least a hundred ships!"

"Possibly two hundred," whispered Matthews in awe.

For my part, all I could say was there were so many ships it was difficult to count them, but I was with Matthews. It looked to me like 200 ships were heading for us.

"Battle stations!" came the command, and I snapped out of my reverie and rushed to the hatchway to take my place on the gundeck. Once more I was assigned to the gun team of Obadiah Jones and Gil Parsons.

When I reached the gun station, Jones looked at me, puzzled. "What are you doing here, young Thomas?" he asked.

"I have been assigned to you, Mr Jones," I said. "Like before, when we were in Cadiz."

Jones shook his head. "You must have missed the last order," he said. "Mr Pugh just sent his mate down. Every fourth man up the rigging to man the sails." He shook his head and spat. "As if it ain't hard enough for us gunners with the few men we have. Ain't that right, Gil?"

"Aye, right enough, Obadiah," agreed Parsons, already ramming the powder into the cannon.

I hurried back up the stairs, to the main deck, and ran into Mr Pugh.

"I am for the sails, sir," I said. "Which one?"

Mr Pugh pointed at the mizen mast. "First spar on the mizen, Thomas, and be quick!" he said.

I ran for the rigging and began to clamber up the rope netting. My stomach was heaving with fear. The height was one thing, but I knew that warships aimed their cannons at the masts and sails of an enemy ship, to disable her in the water.

I climbed higher and higher, hanging on steadfastly to the ropes as the ship swayed. The higher I got, the more difficult it became. I reached the first spar and made my way along it, my hands holding on to the wooden beam and my feet on the rope beneath it.

"Well, well, 'tis my cabin boy!" growled a voice.

I looked along to my right, and there, not a few feet away, was Simnel.

"Looks like Lady Luck has delivered you to me once more," he smirked.

"You would not dare touch me!" I said defiantly, with a courage that I did not really feel. Although I had felt confident about facing Simnel after our last encounter, it was a different matter now, perched on narrow swinging ropes high above the deck of the ship. "You will be seen. We are in full sight of everyone."

"All eyes will be on the battle," leered Simnel. "And a cabin boy falling to his death as the ship rolls, why, he would be just another casualty of war."

"Someone would see you grappling with me," I said.

Simnel shook his head. "They would see what I told them had happened. I saw you about to fall and went to help you, but you slipped from my grasp and fell. A sad thing to happen to a boy so young."

"My uncle would not believe you," I told him angrily.

"Your uncle can believe what he likes," laughed Simnel. "Everyone would say they were just the ravings of a man crazed with grief over the death of his beloved nephew. Why, he already showed how mad he is that last time back in Plymouth, when he unjustly accused me of robbing you in front of Hawkins and the others."

"You did rob me!" I raged. "I know it!"

"Not me, young Thomas," cackled Simnel. "Perhaps friends of mine may have done it, for a price."

"So you admit it!" I said, triumphantly. "Now I have your confession!"

"And much good may it do you," snarled Simnel. "Dead boys tell no tales." And he began to work his way along the spar towards me.

Moving faster than I had ever done before, I backed away from him along the rope and spar, back to the rigging, then shouted to the sailor above, a man I knew: "Mr Taylor, would you swap places with me? I need to see the battle from a greater height."

As Taylor looked down from the next spar up, Simnel stopped moving. It was one thing to hurl me down to the deck when all eyes were on the Spanish ships, it was another to do it when he was being watched.

"Aye," said Taylor, surprised that anyone would want to work higher up the mast in a battle. The higher the position, the greater the danger.

Hastily, I clambered up the rigging as Taylor climbed down, and we changed places.

I could see Simnel's eyes on me, the expression on his face hard and calculating, and I knew that this was just a temporary reprieve. He would be after me again, but he would choose his moment: when the battle was at its fullest heat. I would have to keep my eyes peeled for threats to my life from two directions: one from Spanish cannonballs, and the other from Simnel.

I looked about me and noted that the *Ark* and the *Revenge* had taken position in a column with some of the other English ships. The *Ark* was at the head of the column and our ship second, and we were heading for the first line of Spanish ships. We came in fast towards the nearest one and our guns let off a broadside, hammering cannon-shot into the side of the Spanish galleon, and then immediately our ships turned away before the enemy guns could recover and aim at us. They fired, but most of their shots missed and fell into the sea.

I glanced below, looking for Simnel, but he was nowhere to be seen. Down on deck, Captain Drake and Mr Berry were issuing orders to manoeuvre our ship this way and that, keeping out of range of the

Spanish guns. Then, when the moment was right, we would dart in and let loose another round of cannon-fire, blasting holes in the enemy ships and setting them on fire.

The wind whipped around me as I furled or unfurled the sails as the orders came. All the time I clung on tight, afraid in case I should slip and fall when the ship lurched violently.

Suddenly a figure appeared beside me; Simnel was back.

"Looks a goodly sight from up here, eh, cabin boy?" he asked, laughing.

"It will be your neck hanging on the gallows if you touch me!" I shouted at him. "I will shout murder!"

"And who will hear you with all this cannon-fire below?" sneered Simnel. And with that he reached out for me. I swung myself away from him, but his huge hand grabbed hold of my shirt. "I am afraid you are going to be a casualty of war, my boy," he said. "But I will see your friends get their share of your wages."

He tugged hard at me and I almost fell. Then, as he pulled again, I let go of the spar with one arm, ducked down, and my shirt came half off. I caught the spar rope with my free hand and pulled free of my shirt altogether.

"Play games with me, would you?" snarled Simnel, and he began to shift his feet slowly along the rope towards me.

Just at that second, the *Revenge* turned sharply to starboard and the spar we were on gave a sudden lurch. The force of it hurled Simnel off it. I remember the look of horror on his face as he clutched out at the spar, only to grab at air.

"Help me!" he gasped.

And then he fell, his body falling away from the mast, his arms and hands frantically clutching at ropes that did not exist.

There was a sickening thud from the deck as his body struck the wood below.

Men began to gather round Simnel, whose still body lay at an awkward angle. Some looked up towards me. From just below me Taylor's voice called out: "What happened?"

I was about to explain when the *Revenge* gave another lurch as a Spanish warship opened fire on us. There was an explosion just off our starboard side and water poured over the deck.

"Haul up the mizen sails!" came the cry, and I climbed back up to my position on the spar and set to work with the others, hauling on the rope that pulled up the sail. Glancing down, I saw two sailors carrying Simnel's body away below decks.

There was very little time for me to dwell on what had just happened. The Spanish ships began to pour cannon-fire at us, and all our efforts were needed to make the *Revenge* turn this way and that to keep out of range, while at the same time returning fire. I hauled and slackened ropes until my shoulders ached and I felt my arms would be torn out of their sockets.

The rest of that day the battle raged. As darkness fell the signal flags went up on the *Ark* giving us orders to disengage from the Spanish ships and head for our own waters.

I came down from the rigging and discovered that the Spanish fleet had suffered so much damage that they had retreated further out into the Channel. Perhaps they were hoping to tempt the English ships closer, within reach of their guns, but Admiral Howard had decided to keep our fleet safe for the night.

I sought out Uncle Rufus and Stevens and told them what had happened to Simnel, and how he had fallen trying to throw me from the spar.

"The villain!" scowled Rufus. "He got his just deserts in the end!"

"Aye," nodded Stevens, "and perhaps 'tis best to

leave it as it is. Let the story be that he lost his grip during the battle and fell. A casualty of war."

"Aye," nodded Rufus. "Let there be an end to it. 'Tis in the past, Thomas. Simnel is dead and you are alive, and that is all that matters."

But I could not keep another thought from surfacing in my brain. What if someone had seen what had happened between Simnel and myself up in the rigging? What if I were blamed for his death and they called it murder? Murderers were hanged, and I imagined myself hanging at the end of a rope, just like those criminals I had seen in London.

That night I was so tired I sank on to my sacking and fell straight to sleep. In the middle of the night I awoke from a nightmare, in which I felt Simnel grabbing at my throat, and then saw him falling again. I must have been muttering fitfully in my sleep about him, because as I woke I found Rufus looking gently down at me.

"There there, Thomas," he said. "Simnel's dead and gone now. He cannot hurt you any more. Just get back to sleep. You are going to need your strength tomorrow."

I nodded, and lay down, and soon I heard Rufus snoring beside me. The next thing I remember is waking to urgent shouts of "Battle stations!" being called throughout the lower decks.

I hurried up to the deck with Rufus and the rest of the men. Dawn was just coming up, but already the Spanish ships were forming up for another attack.

Once again, I climbed the rigging to the spar across the mizen mast to take my place on the sail. We were heading for the lines of enemy ships, just as before. As we approached them, we turned broadside to fire a volley of cannon-shot, then turned again and headed inshore.

"The Captain's got them where he wants them!" chuckled Taylor from beside me. "See how he moves us out of range every time the Spanish come for us. And then he turns us back and we attack again."

"Captain Drake is a fine sailor," I agreed.

"The finest," said Taylor. With his free hand he pointed at the deck of the nearest Spanish ship which was busy with armed soldiers, and sailors holding ropes with hooks. "See that?" he said. "Them Spaniards with their ropes? They hope we will come close enough for their soldiers to board us. They want to battle at close quarters. But Captain Drake's too

137

wily for 'em. Keep 'em at a distance till he is ready for 'em, that is his way."

The battle continued in this fashion for hours, with myself and the men along the spars raising and lowering the sails, following orders from the men at each end of the spar. Then I saw one of the Spanish ships, the *Rosario*, break away and head for the English coast. Suddenly, the *Revenge* changed course and we began to head for the breakaway Spanish ship. At the same time three other of our ships, the *Roebuck* and two smaller vessels, joined us in giving chase. It seemed a strange course of action for the *Rosario* to take. I did not know whether some accident had befallen the ship, or its captain was determined to be the first to land on English soil, even if it cost him his ship and his life. If it had been a considered course of action, it was a foolhardy one by the Spanish captain, because in no time at all our ship and the three other English ships had surrounded the *Rosario* like hounds on a fox.

Cannon-fire came from our gundecks, and those of the *Roebuck*, and from my high position I saw fires break out on the deck of the Spanish ship. Almost immediately, the *Rosario* furled her sails and a white flag was run up her masthead. A great cheer went up from all of us. Our first prize of the battle!

As we drew alongside the captured Spanish ship, I watched Rufus and Stevens go with the boarding party. That night, when we had moved nearer shore with the rest of the English fleet, I learned just how big a prize we had taken.

"Nothing less than 52,000 ducats in gold!" Uncle Rufus told me delightedly.

"And her hold crammed with silver plate and jewels," added Stevens.

"She is surely the paymaster ship for the whole Spanish Armada!" laughed Rufus. "I have never seen so much treasure on board one ship afore! Not even the *San Felipe*!"

"With so much precious loot on board, I wonder why she broke away and headed for the shore?" I said, baffled. "Her captain must have known she was bound to be captured."

"Who knows?" shrugged Stevens. "Though I do not doubt that the Spanish captain will be telling Captain Drake his reasons over a bottle of fine wine."

I looked at them, puzzled. "But I thought the *Rosario* and its crew had been taken into Torbay under command of the *Roebuck*?"

"Aye, 'tis so," nodded Rufus. "But not before its

cargo and Captain had been brought aboard. A Spanish lord of a captain will make a fine and expensive hostage for all of us. Captain Drake will want to keep him in good shape so he gets a good price for him after all this is over."

That night there was much rejoicing on board at the great prize we had captured. The crew were issued with an extra tot of rum, though I declined mine. The smell of it reminded me too much of Simnel's foul breath. As I watched Rufus, Stevens, Jones, Parsons and the rest of the crew singing and dancing on the lower deck, I felt a tap on my shoulder. I turned and found myself looking into the unsmiling face of Mr Pugh.

"I want a word with you, boy," he said. "About the death of Mr Simnel. Follow me."

My heart sank. I realized that in some way he must have discovered the truth about Simnel's fall. That it had not been an accident, but that it had come about because he had fought with me in the rigging. I wondered if one of Simnel's friends had reported it with a different slant to it, perhaps even saying that I had pushed him.

I followed Mr Pugh up the stairs to the upper deck. At the top he turned and fixed me with a grim look.

Before he could speak, I blurted out, "I did not kill him, Mr Pugh!"

"Then tell me what did happen, boy."

As briefly as I could I told him everything that had happened: my being robbed, Simnel's treatment of Jamie, his threats to me, and finally his attempts to throw me from the spar.

Mr Pugh listened in silence. When I had finished, he nodded and said, "What you say has the ring of truth, young Hobbs. I always thought Simnel to be a villain, but in times of war we need men, and often we cannot choose the kind of men they are. But this ship has a fine reputation, as does its crew. We do not want stories spread that might reflect badly on those reputations. Do you understand what I am saying, boy?"

I thought it over, and then nodded. "I think you are telling me it would be best if we say Simnel died because of the war."

"Exactly that," said Mr Pugh. "He died during the course of a Spanish attack. He died a hero, as did all the other men who died defending their country. Do you agree?"

I held my tongue. Simnel, the coward, the bully, was to be a hero of the war. It was a bitter pill to swallow, but I knew that Mr Pugh was right, it was the only course of action to take for the good of the rest of the crew.

I nodded. "Yes, Mr Pugh," I said.

"Good," he said.

*August 1588*

For the next week we kept up our attacks on the Spanish fleet, sailing into battle each day just before dawn and hammering them with our cannon-fire. Spanish ship after Spanish ship was being wrecked, but with little cost to our own fleet. The whole time we were pushing the enemy ships eastwards, chasing and harassing the Armada towards Kent, where another part of our fleet was waiting for them off the coast. They eventually turned away from England and headed for the French coast and the port of Calais. We continued to give chase until, on 6th August, the signal flags went up from the Lord Admiral's ship for us to withdraw back and stand ready in case the Spanish should suddenly make another dash for the English coast.

I stood at our port rail with the other crewmen, watching the Spanish ships in the harbour at Calais. Even from a distance we could see that many of them were heavily damaged, with burn marks blackening their paintwork, and great gaping holes in their sides.

"We've got 'em bottled up now, boys," said one crewman with satisfaction.

Later that afternoon, the orders for attack were issued amongst us. It was a bold plan. At midnight, when the tide turned and it would be running fast towards the French coast, fireships would be launched, aimed directly at the enemy fleet. If the Spanish ships stayed where they were, they would be burnt. If they came out of harbour to escape the blazing hulks, we would be waiting for them.

As the afternoon light faded, I watched one of the fireships being prepared. It was the 200-ton *Thomas*, one of the ships from Captain Drake's own personal fleet. All along the top deck, sheaves of wooden faggots were being laid out, with pitch being poured over them to ensure a good fire when the ship began to burn. The gunpowder and guns were left below on the gundecks, to guarantee a massive explosion, with the cannons left fully loaded to add to it. The same was happening on another seven ships. Eight fireships in all, aimed at burning the Armada.

When the *Thomas* had been fully prepared, Mr Belson came over to where Rufus, Stevens and I were standing.

"Ready, Rufus?" he asked.

144

"Aye, all ready, Mr Belson," nodded Rufus.

Stevens and I looked at him, puzzled.

Rufus gave a shy smile. "I did not want to tell you before in case you got jealous," he said. "Only I heard that Captain Drake was looking for volunteers to man the fireships." He looked at the *Thomas*, now a floating bomb tied up alongside us.

I gaped. "You?" I said.

Stevens looked angry. "You did not tell me, Rufus. Your oldest friend!"

"Nay, you would have only wanted it for yourself," said Rufus. "Or tried to talk me out of it." He looked down at the *Thomas* again, a fond look on his face. "I sailed on her many years ago. 'Tis only fitting I should be the one to say a final goodbye to her."

Stevens fell silent, his face as impassive as ever, but I could see the pain in his eyes. He held out his hand. "Good luck, Rufus," he said. "Come back safely."

"I will, old friend," said Rufus, and he shook Stevens's hand.

Then Rufus turned to me. "If I do not survive this night, Thomas, I have told Mr Belson to get the purser to give you my wages for this venture. You are to give it to your father, as payment for all the meals I have had at his table."

I felt a lump in my throat, and was doing my best to stop myself crying. "A penny would cover all the meals you have had at our house," I said.

"Nay, do not be hard," he grinned. "Your father means well."

"'Tis time, Rufus," said Mr Belson.

Rufus nodded. "I am with you, Mr Belson," he said.

And then they walked away. Soon I saw Rufus go over the rail and clamber down a rope ladder, and land on the deck of the fireship. Then he waved, and went down below the deck of the doomed ship.

"Come away, Thomas," said Stevens with a sigh. "'Twill be a long wait before midnight and the tide turns. Your uncle will need that time to prepare himself, and us watching him will do him no good."

I knew that Stevens was right, but my heart felt heavy.

"What will happen?" I asked. "How will he get off once it is burning?"

"He has a small boat tied to it. Once the hulk gets close enough to the French coast that Rufus is sure the tide and wind will take it in, he will set fire to the trails of pitch and tar that have been laid. When the fire is well alight, he will get down into the boat and row back here."

"But say the pitch burns too fast? Or he gets trapped?"

Stevens did not say anything, just looked thoughtful. And then he walked away.

As darkness fell and night drew in, I could not help but return to the side of the ship and look at the *Thomas*. In the moonlight I could see Rufus moving about on the old ship. Other men had joined him. These, I was told, would be the few crew who would help him get the boat under way. They would leave once the boat was heading well for Calais.

Midnight came, and in the dark the *Thomas* was pushed off from the *Revenge*. I watched the whole time and wondered if Stevens would come and join me at the rail, but there was no sign of him. Apart from Stevens, the whole crew seemed to be there to see it leave. I even saw Captain Drake himself, watching from the fo'c'sle.

I heard the flap of the fireship's sails as the ship caught the night wind, then it soon disappeared into the darkness, heading for the coast of France.

We waited, and after about fifteen minutes I heard a faint splash.

"They are dropping a longboat," said one sailor near me. "Sending back the others."

I heard the sound of oars in the water, dipping in and out, quietly, and then I saw the longboat appear out of the darkness and come alongside. One by one the men who had helped Rufus take the *Thomas* out on its initial journey came up the rope ladder. The last to appear was Stevens.

"Stevens!" I exclaimed.

"I wanted to help Rufus at least on part of his journey," he said simply. Then he joined me by the rail, and we watched.

In the distance we saw the darkness lit by a small flame. Then, a bit further away, another. Then another. The fireships were being set alight.

"Come on, Rufus," Stevens whispered urgently beside me. "Do not hang about, old friend."

The flames spread, and soon there was a series of burning beacons sailing on the sea. As I watched the fires grew larger and larger, flames now running along the decks of the fireships, the mast and riggings visible in their glow. The sails of one of the ships caught alight, and soon a sheet of flame was soaring up into the night sky. One by one, the other fireships followed suit.

"Come on, Rufus! Leave!" muttered Stevens urgently again.

Eight ships were now seen, clearly ablaze, heading straight on the tide towards the port of Calais and the anchored Spanish fleet. For the Spanish it must have been a terrifying sight, like Hell on water come to devour them.

"That will bring them out, or they will burn in Damnation!" I heard the voice of Captain Drake shout.

A cheer went up from our crew, but all I could do was worry about Uncle Rufus. The fireships moved further and further away from us. "They must be in Calais by now," said Stevens grimly.

And then we heard the first explosions. Flame filled the night air. In the distance, in the light from the flames, I could make out the movement of the Spanish ships as they fled from their moorings, desperate to escape from the fireships. Once again, the Spanish fleet were at sea, at our mercy.

Amid the cheering from our men and the explosions from the harbour, I heard a scrabbling from the rail as the rope ladder near to me went taut. Stevens heard it, too. He rushed to the rail and leaned over, just as Uncle Rufus clambered into view.

My heart felt filled with joy as he grinned at me.

"Well, Thomas," he said, "looks like your dad will not get my wages after all."

The fireship attack at Calais spelled the end of the Armada. The Spanish ships were forced out of their safe harbour and tried to head east to Dunkirk, but our fleet caught them at Gravelines, halfway between Calais and Dunkirk, and they were devastated by our cannon. The last we saw of the ships that survived, they were sailing east rather than heading west back to Spain, towards more of our fleet.

## Epilogue

### September 1588

Just in case the Spanish ships returned, our fleet stayed in the Channel for another month. Then in September we got word that the remains of the Armada had hit a storm off the west coast of Ireland that wrecked most of the remaining ships. The Armada had been destroyed, and my time at sea – for this occasion – had come to an end.

When it came time for me to collect my pay, I took no chances at being robbed again, but asked Rufus and Stevens to accompany me back to London. With my wages and the profits from the prizes we had taken, especially the *Rosario*, I had 70 shillings as my pay. I planned to give my dad and mam 50, and keep 20 for myself.

It was with a feeling of sadness that I left Plymouth with Rufus and Stevens. The most exciting time of my life had just ended for me, and I wondered if anything would ever be as thrilling again. Filled with these sad thoughts, I must have made poor company on the journey back to London. Once we reached Moorgate, I bade Rufus and Stevens farewell, promising to meet up with them later, and finally made my return home.

My arrival back at Garlands was very different from my last. This time I had come home with my pockets filled with money, as I had always said I would. As I offered the 50 shillings to my dad he stunned me by saying, "Keep the money, Thomas. 'Tis yours."

I felt anger rising up in my throat. Here was I, offering him more money than he had ever held in his hand, and he was throwing it back in my face, just for spite. I was just about to tell him this angrily, when he added in a quiet voice: "I have been unfair to you, Thomas. I thought you would never amount to anything, especially going off with your uncle. But I was wrong. You left here a boy and you have come back as a man in your own right. It would be wrong of me to take money from you."

There was an awkward silence in the room. Then Mam said, "John, I think you and Thomas have more to say to one another." With that she took Mary and young Daniel into the small room.

My dad looked at me, and then he said, "Your mam wants me to say I am sorry for everything that I have said, but I cannot. I am not sorry. I was worried about you. First I was worried you would not be able to look after yourself but would depend too much on me and your mam. Then I was worried in case you became a vagabond and a wastrel as happens so often with sailors. As I say, I am heartily relieved that neither has happened and you have grown into a proper man, but I am not sorry I said those things."

All that time I had spent thinking Dad didn't care about me, but his harsh words were his way of caring. I thought it had just been about the money. Now, he had proved to me that the money had never been his main concern.

"Dad," I said, "please, take this money. If not for you, then for Mam and Mary and Daniel. And even though I am now a man in my own right, in your heart let me always be your boy. For you will always be my father, and much loved."

Dad hesitated, and then he held out his arms to me and, for the first time in many long years, he hugged me. I felt like I had my dad back once more.

Using my 50 shillings, we were finally able to achieve Dad's dream and move into a small house of our own, though still within the walls of the City of London. Four separate rooms and our own outside privy! I felt like a Lord of the Manor!

For the moment, I go out with my friend William and enjoy the entertainments of London, but am careful not to let all and sundry know I have money put away in a safe place. I wait for the day that Rufus will call on us again, and say that we are wanted – that Captain Drake has a place for us on board his next voyage. Because I know now, that is where I belong. The sea.

# Historical note

The attempted invasion of England by the Spanish Armada in 1588 was just one aspect of the war between Spain and England. At its core, the war was about religion: Catholic versus Protestant.

The trouble began when Henry VIII's first wife, Catherine of Aragon, did not produce the male heir he wanted. Henry asked the Pope for a divorce from Catherine, but the Pope refused. Between 1532 and 1536 Henry passed a series of Acts of Parliament replacing the Pope with himself as Head of the Church in England. Henry divorced Catherine and in 1533 married Anne Boleyn. (He later married a further four times.) After Henry VIII's death in 1547 he was succeeded by his son, Edward VI, who became King of England at just 10 years old, and died at the age of 15. During Edward's short reign the Reformation of the English Church, begun by Henry VIII, continued and the English Church adopted Protestantism and rejected Catholicism.

Edward VI was succeeded by his half-sister, Mary

(Catherine of Aragon's daughter), who was half Spanish and a devout Catholic. She married the future King Philip II of Spain. During their marriage, Philip remained mostly in Spain while Mary ruled England. Mary was determined to return England to the Church of Rome. To enforce this she carried out a systematic persecution of Protestants, burning those who refused to adopt the Catholic faith. About 380 Protestants in England were burnt to death, including Archbishop Thomas Cranmer. This gave her the nickname "Bloody Mary".

After Mary's death in 1558, her half-sister Elizabeth became Queen of England. Elizabeth had spent much of Mary's reign as a prisoner in the Tower of London, because Mary was concerned that Elizabeth might be the focus for a Protestant revolution.

In 1563 Elizabeth created the Church of England, based on the 39 Articles. This automatically turned English Catholics into traitors and brought her into conflict with the Catholic nations and the Catholic Church. The Pope and King Philip of Spain in particular wanted England brought back into the Catholic religion. Relations between England and Spain were made worse by their rivalry in seizing new territories across the world.

Spain had conquered much of South America, while North America had been claimed by Sir Walter Raleigh for England. And there were many other rich lands that both countries laid claim to.

Hostilities between Protestant England and Catholic Spain continued to escalate, and were made even worse following Elizabeth's execution of the Catholic Mary Queen of Scots in 1587. (The Scottish Queen had been part of a plot to overthrow Elizabeth and replace her with Mary on the English throne.) News reached Elizabeth that a Spanish Armada was being assembled in Cadiz, and was being made ready to invade England. The Queen ordered Sir Francis Drake and a small fleet to destroy it, which he did in a very successful surprise attack. However, in 1588, a much larger Armada was assembled, partly funded by the Pope. This was the fleet that was to carry the invading army intended to overrun England and return it to Catholic control.

The Spanish Armada, consisting of 130 ships and 31,000 men and commanded by the Duke Medina Sidonia, left Lisbon in Portugal for England on 29th May 1588. Before it set out, Pope Sixtus V offered a reward of a million ducats if the Spanish succeeded in overthrowing Elizabeth.

Storms delayed the progress of the Armada, causing problems with supplies, and by 19th June it had only managed to get to Corunna on the north-west of Spain. The Armada finally left Corunna on 22nd July, having been refitted, but already having lost some 4,000 men due to desertion or disease.

The plan was for the Armada to sail along the French coast of the English Channel until it reached Dunkirk. Here it was to rendezvous with the main Spanish invasion force under the Duke of Parma, and take them across the Channel to invade England.

As soon as word of the Armada reached England, preparations were made to defend the whole length of the south coast. A fleet of sixteen warships was based at Queenborough (in Kent, at the mouth of the Thames). Nine warships under Sir Henry Palmer cruised the Narrow Seas (the Straits of Dover), and three warships based at Plymouth under Sir Francis Drake (the *Revenge*, the *Hope* and the *Nonpareil*) guarded the western approaches. They were accompanied by many smaller ships.

When the Armada approached the English coast off the south-west it was attacked and harried so fiercely by the English ships that it had no chance to get near the coast. The Spanish ships sought refuge in the

French ports of Calais, but the English used fireships to force the Spanish ships back out to sea. The English fleet then attacked the Spanish fleet at Gravelines, off the French coast halfway between Calais and Dunkirk, and severely damaged the Armada.

Nearly all the Spanish ships were in very bad condition by the time they reached Dunkirk, but their hope was that they would take on board the Duke of Parma's waiting army, and so still be able to carry out the invasion plan. In actual fact, Parma's troops were far from ready, and the invasion was abandoned.

Both men blamed the other: Medina Sidonia claimed that there was no invasion army ready at Dunkirk to be transported to England; Parma claimed that the problem lay with the Spanish ships not being ready to transport his men.

The truth seems to be that the planned invading army had not been assembled by the Duke of Parma, despite his letters of assurance to King Philip of Spain informing him that "my men are ready". It is believed that Parma never had any intention of carrying out the invasion, but went along with it because he believed the Armada would never get as far as it did.

After this debacle, the Armada continued on past the tip of south-east England, then sailed north. The strong English defences, both by ships and sea-defences on land, meant they were unable to land at any point, and with no invading army on board anyway, any attempt at landing was futile. The Armada continued on around the coast of Scotland, and then back south, passing Ireland. Off the west coast of Ireland it hit a storm that wrecked many of the Spanish boats.

However, the destruction of the Armada did not mean the end of the war between Spain and England; the war continued for another fifteen years with further battles at sea between the ships of both countries.

In August 1591 the *Revenge* was part of a squadron of six under the command of Lord Thomas Howard which mounted a blockade in the mid-Atlantic to stop Spanish ships bringing silver back from the Americas. When Howard received news that a huge and powerful Spanish fleet was on its way, he ordered the squadron to retreat. Five of the ships got away, but the *Revenge* was bringing up the rear and was surrounded by the Spanish. In the fierce battle that ensued, the *Revenge* was lost. Legend has it that the Captain, Sir Richard Grenville, realising that escape was impossible, ordered that the ship to be sunk rather than let it fall into enemy hands.

Sir Francis Drake died in January 1596 from dysentery and was buried at sea near Nombre de Dios in the West Indies. He was almost 50 years old. Lord Howard remained Lord High Admiral well into the reign of James I (who succeeded Elizabeth I). He resigned his post in 1619 at the age of 83, and died in 1623 at the age of 87.

# Timeline

**1532–6** Henry VIII introduces a series of laws replacing the Pope with the English monarch as head of the English Church.

**1547–53** England ruled by Edward VI (who dies at the age of 15). During his reign the English Church adopts Protestantism and breaks with the Roman Catholic Church.

**1553–1558** Reign of Mary I. Catholic faith reintroduced to England by force, 380 Protestants burned to death for refusing to adopt the Catholic faith.

**1558** Elizabeth I ascends to the throne.

**1563** The Church of England created, based on the 39 Articles. This automatically turns English Catholics into traitors.

**1568** Unsuccessful Scottish plot against Elizabeth aimed at putting the Catholic Mary Queen of Scots on the English throne and uniting England and Scotland. Mary imprisoned in England.

**1570** Pope Pius V issues a proclamation urging the

assassination of Queen Elizabeth. Over the next decade a series of plans are drawn up by Spain and the Pope to assassinate Elizabeth and invade England.

**1586** Spanish-backed Babington Plot to assassinate Elizabeth and replace her on the English throne with Mary Queen of Scots uncovered. This to be backed with invasion of England by Spain. Conspirators arrested. Spanish ambassador expelled to France.

**February 1587** Execution of Mary Queen of Scots. Pope Sixtus V issues a reward of one million ducats to be paid when Elizabeth is overthrown and a Catholic monarch once more rules England. Intelligence obtained that Spanish invasion fleet is assembling in Cadiz.

**April 1587** Drake's fleet attacks the Spanish fleet at Cadiz and destroys it.

**1588** A new and larger Spanish fleet – the Spanish Armada – sets sail to invade England. Defeated by the English navy, and by bad weather.

**1596** Drake dies.

**1597** A second Armada sent by Philip of Spain to invade England is destroyed by storms.

**1598** King Philip II of Spain dies.

**1603** Elizabeth I dies.

*Sir Francis Drake.*

*Cross-section sketch of Drake's ship, the Revenge. The gundeck with its cannons can be seen in the centre of the ship.*

*Philip II of Spain.*

*Elizabeth I in a portrait celebrating the defeat of the Armada, which is illustrated in the scenes behind the Queen.*

*Map showing the Spanish fleet off the south-west coast of England.*

*A sea-battle between the English and Spanish fleets in the English Channel.*

*Armada treasure – gold coins found in the shipwrecked Spanish galleon Girona.*

*A navigation instrument found off the Irish coast probably from the wreck of a Spanish Armada galleon.*

*Scene from on board the Revenge during its last battle with the Spanish in 1591.*

*Elizabeth I riding through the streets of London to St Paul's Cathedral, where she gave thanks to God for sending the winds that scattered the Armada.*

# Picture acknowledgements

**P164**      Sir Francis Drake, Topham Picturepoint

**P165**      Cross-section sketch of the Revenge, Topham Picturepoint

**P166**      Philip II of Spain by Sir Anthonis Mor (Antonio Moro), Prado, Madrid, Spain/Bridgeman Art Library

**P167**      Elizabeth I, Armada portrait, Private Collection/Bridgeman Art Library

**P168**      Map showing the Spanish Armada, Topham Picturepoint

**P169**      Spanish fleet dispersed by fireships, Mary Evans Picture Library

**P170**      Gold coins found in Galleon Girona, Topham Picturepoint

**P171**      Mariners astrolobe, Topham Picturepoint

**P172**      Sir Richard Grenville on the Revenge, Topham Picturepoint

**P173**      Elizabeth I rides to St Paul's Cathedral, Mary Evans Picture Library